Queen for a Night

Donna Keeley

DEDICATION

To everyone who read the first book and told me,
"I can't wait to read the next book."
You are my inspiration.
Thank you for your patience.

ACKNOWLEDGMENTS

I want to acknowledge the incredible help I've received for these first two books, and hopefully all the rest to follow.

Firstly, to my wonderful editor, Martin Roy Hill, who is also a gifted writer of thrillers and has extensive experience as a newspaper man, government contractor, and cat lover. These books would not be half as good without his input.

Secondly, to my cover artist, Megan Katsanevakis, who understands the "look" I'm trying to achieve and has rendered my vision into a reality, including making Styx come to life.

INTRODUCTION

Hi. My name is Shannon MacIntyre and I talk to ghosts. No, really. I do.

Before I started talking to ghosts, I was an investigative reporter with a much-loved, high stress job. That resulted in a heart attack at age thirty-eight and I died. Briefly. When they revived me, I was sent to recover at my sister's house in Idyllwild, California. While I was there my dead grandmother appeared to tell me that I could now speak to the spirits. She said I had a duty to help them because of my "gift."

This is one of those gifts that keeps on giving. And not necessarily in a good way.

My first use of my power, gift, quirk—whatever you want to call it—was solving a mystery at the Whaley House in San Diego, California. The ghosts were upset that something was stolen, and I had to get it back. Which I did, but I was almost shot. However, that's another story. Literally.

Immediately after I helped the Whaley ghosts, I was contacted by a retired Silicon Valley billionaire who runs a paranormal site. He has the same "gift," or something similar, and he knows when things happen—and where. We have a sort of partnership going. He lets me know where the hot spots are, and I check them out. I get to do a write-up for his site and get paid. But I don't use my real name because I worked too hard as a journalist to build my reputation and get to where I was at a major newspaper in Chicago. Also, my peers would never let me hear the end of it. But pseudonyms work just as well.

My investigative skills are useful in these cases and for the most part no one dies, probably because most of them are already dead. Oh, and I now have this cat named Styx who goes with me everywhere. He's actually pretty smart, and I sometimes wonder if there is more to him than meets the eye.

Basically, even though I do this very weird job, I'm cynical and sarcastic and I don't take everything at face value. I like to dig around and uncover things, especially if it's something that needs to be exposed. I don't always like what I find, but that's beside the point.

CHAPTER 1

"Look, I'm sorry. Okay?" I spoke around the bloody finger stuck in my mouth. I was in my room back at my sister's house and Styx was under the bed. He was extremely pissed. I could hear the swish of his tail lashing back and forth on the hardwood floor.

"I told you he wouldn't like it," my nephew, Jared, warned me from the doorway.

I nodded. "Yes. You were right. I should have listened."

"Want me to get a broom and I can chase him out from under the bed?" he offered excitedly in that typical seven-year-old male way. Anything that could be used as a weapon was a good thing.

"No thanks." I removed my finger from my mouth; the bleeding had slowed. "I can get him out with a treat or something."

"Oh." The disappointment was evident. "Alright." He turned away.

"Close the door so he doesn't get out, okay Jared? Thanks."

The door shut. Styx and I were alone. A grumbling, growling noise came from under the bed. There was some thrashing and a bright green collar with a tag came flying out, landing near my feet. Message received.

"I said I was sorry. I promise I'll never try to put that on you again. I was just thinking you needed some identification in case you got lost." I grabbed a tissue from the dispenser beside my bed and wrapped it around my injured digit.

He huffed as if the idea was ludicrous. I'm sure in his opinion, it was.

"Gimme a break, I've never been a pet owner before. I thought that's what people do."

I was exasperated, in pain, and tired of fighting with a seven-pound adversary. It had taken my sister's two kids and me a lot of wrestling to get the collar on him while we were down in the living room, and his response was to explode in a ball of fur and claws at this intrusion on his person. Fortunately, I was the only one hurt. He had bolted upstairs to our room with Jared and me following, my niece Karen wisely staying out of the chase. My bloody finger was a reminder of how wrong I had been. I sat heavily on the bed.

After a few moments he emerged. He sat at my feet with his ears back, glaring at me. He wanted to make very sure I understood.

"For the third time, I'm sorry. We all make mistakes. That's part of being human."

He seemed to accept the apology and jumped up on the bed, making sure to keep out of arm's reach. I didn't move. I was too tired.

Since my return from San Diego, I was trying to take it easy. I was still recuperating from my heart attack and my involvement in the Whaley House mystery was not exactly stress-free. A nap before dinner sounded good so I repositioned myself on the bed to lie down.

I closed my eyes and relaxed. Unfortunately, sleep didn't come right away. My mind was whirring away replaying the events of the past week. I had returned, triumphant, from my trip to San Diego. I had a mysterious benefactor who was paying me to write exclusively for his web site. And I was ten thousand dollars richer.

Cyrus Winston was a retired Silicon Valley billionaire who had an interest in the paranormal. He had called right after I solved the Whaley House case and offered to fund my investigations. It all seemed surreal when I thought about it, though the promised money had landed in my bank account with no problems.

As I finally drifted off, I could faintly hear Styx purring from the end of the bed. Apparently, I was forgiven.

My nap was far from the restful break I was hoping for. My dreams were weird and disjointed, the images overlapping each other and making no sense. I was on a cruise ship and I could hear the rough ocean waves crashing against the hull. In another scene I peered down the dark hallways of the engineering section that seemed miles long and very fuzzy. Now loud engine noises made it impossible to hear anything else. I floated up through the decks to the passenger area where the polished woods, the artwork, expansive lounges, and carefully crafted rooms were a testament to the Art Deco period. A variety of people from different eras of the twentieth century passed before me—upper class passengers in tuxedos and evening gowns from the 1930s, 40s, and 50s, dancing gaily in the ballroom and eating in elaborate dining rooms. Other classes of passengers appeared, a little less elegant but still enjoying themselves in their surroundings. Lots of music, drinking, and smoking. I felt myself involuntarily cringe as I smelled the tobacco smoke from cigarettes, cigars, and pipes.

Then the picture changed, and I saw soldiers in their gear lined up in the hallways, standing shoulder-to-shoulder, and eating in a much less glamorous environment. Rows upon rows of bunk beds, three high, covered every available space in the cabins, the lounges, and even in the swimming pool. The decks were packed with people standing together against the railings in drab uniforms. Such a contrast to the light and color before.

Suddenly there was an impact, and I physically shook. The sound of tearing metal, rushing water, and screams pulled me out of the vision harshly. Groggy and uncertain of where I was, I knew it was more than just a dream and that I would definitely remember these images for some time to come.

I pulled myself into a sitting position as I heard Lillith coming up the stairs. She knocked gently on my door. "Come in," I croaked.

"Did I wake you?" she seemed concerned when she saw me in the bed.

"No, I just got up from a nap."

"I see he's forgiven you," she nodded at Styx curled up by my feet, his favorite spot.

"Not completely. He's making sure to stay out of reach. I really ticked him off with that collar."

"Well, we really don't know much about him. He just showed up a couple of months before you did. Maybe someone tried to strangle him and that's why he doesn't like collars. People can be so mean to cats, especially black ones." She strode over and petted him. He looked up at her and purred. "He certainly is very trusting guy. I guess you're officially a pet owner now." She smiled at me.

"Whodathunkit," I replied. "Certainly not anyone who knows me." I laughed. Styx got to his feet, stretched languidly, and strolled over to rub against me. I put my hand on his head and scratched. "Am I finally forgiven?" I asked him.

He mewed quietly and jumped off the bed to head downstairs.

My sister laughed. "I guess so," she surmised. "I came up to tell you that dinner is almost done, and I could use some extra hands if you're up to it."

I nodded and stood up. "Sure. Let me wash the sleep out of my eyes and I'll be right down."

"Thanks," she said, heading back down the stairs.

Cold water helped me to wake up more, but the visions were still there. They were so clear and distinct I knew that they held meaning for me. Exactly what kind of meaning I couldn't tell, but I was sure they would be useful when the time was right. For the moment, I pushed them to the back of my mind and went downstairs to help Lillith.

"Can you help set the table?" she asked once we were in the kitchen. "The guests will be arriving soon." My sister had bought our grandparents' old house and ran a bed-and-breakfast in Idyllwild, California with her husband and children. I had been recuperating with them after my heart attack and she had nursed me back to health, like a good big sister. Since I was taking up one of the rooms used for guests, I always tried to help out where I could.

I nodded to her and headed to the dining room where our grandmother's china was kept. I had barely reached the kitchen door when she called to me from her position at the stove.

"Oh, I almost forgot. You got a phone call a while ago. I thought you were outside with Jared, so I took a message. It's rather cryptic though."

"How so?" I asked.

"It's just a few words. It's like the person who called knew you would understand. I left it by the phone for you."

"Okay. I'll look at it after I get the dishes on the table."

In the large dining room, I opened the massive oak china cabinet that took up almost one entire wall. A marble serving board stretched the length of it which Lilleth used as a buffet, setting out the serving bowls and platters so people could serve themselves. It was a testament to a time of hand-crafted, good-quality work. The cabinet had come with the house when my grandfather bought it and my grandmother made good use of it for her family. I carefully removed placemats, silverware, glasses, plates, and dishes from it.

Lilleth loved using the good china because it was part of the house and of our childhood. People who stayed here were always impressed by the table she set. It was such a Victorian touch in our fast-paced, disposable, modern world. I was always amazed by her loyalty to this side of the family and her dedication to preserving traditions. I know Nana Mac was pleased with her. In fact, I knew it directly from the source.

There were only two couples staying as guests and I quickly set the table for all attending. Nana Mac's service could easily handle twenty, and the table had inserts to accommodate that many. If my grandparents had stayed in Scotland, where they were born, then the entire set could have been used because they both came from large, extended families. But when they decided to move to America, the extended family was left behind and it was only the two of them with their three children—my father, my Uncle Andy, and my Aunt Marilyn. Grandpa Mac had joked that it cost more to ship her china from Scotland to California than it did to pay for their trans-Atlantic passage from Glasgow to New York.

Once the last glass was placed, I went into the hallway where the phone sat in its special alcove to retrieve the abbreviated message. The original phone in the house had been a large box of wood mounted on the wall with a crank on the side. The current phone was small, portable, and included an answering machine in the base. Ah, progress.

The little pink message paper was right beside the machine. It read:

LONG BEACH. QUEEN MARY. ASAP.

Lillith was correct. I did understand the strange message. It was from Cyrus Winston and corresponded with my recent dream. The As Soon As Possible part was annoying to me. I couldn't exactly drop everything and leave at once, and I certainly didn't intend to.

I stuffed the note into my pocket and returned to the dining room china cabinet for the serving pieces to take into the kitchen for the food. Even with hand washing the dishes, Lillith didn't skimp, and presented her meals using everything from the set. One of those touches that made her business stand out from the rest.

Dinner with guests was always an interesting affair with grown-up conversation around the table. My journalistic instincts had me asking the "W" questions—Who, What, Where, When, Why, and How—to learn more about people

who were staying here. Yes, I know How is spelled with an
"H" but reporters still count it because it's important for
information gathering. The kids always ate earlier in the
kitchen since my sister and her husband were the type of
parents who understood that listening to a bunch of adults
talk was the most boring activity on the planet for them.

After the meal and lending a hand to dry all the dishes, I
found I was tired enough to retire to my room for the
evening. The lure of having some time on the internet before
it got bogged down with the kids watching YouTube or Dan
playing an online game was beckoning. I had completely
forgotten about the message from Winston.

I was reminded of my summons as I was getting ready for
bed. I had removed my jeans and was folding them for
wearing the next day when the pink message paper fell from
the pocket as I held the pants upside down. I picked it up off
the floor and contemplated it, wondering why my benefactor
hadn't used my cell phone to contact me. I briefly wondered
how he got the phone number for the house then had a
"duh" moment remembering this was a business. But still, my
cell phone would have been more direct.

Curious, I opened the drawer in the bed side table and
took my phone out. It was a typical flip-phone of the time—
considered "old" by current technology standards, but it
served its purpose. I opened it and looked at the blank screen.
It was dead.

I pressed the power button. Still dead.

I plugged it into the charger. Continued dead.

After twenty minutes of charging there was still no sign of
life. This wasn't one of those the-battery-has-run-out dead,
this was it-would-never-work-again dead.

Believe me, I know dead.

I sighed, highly annoyed. Shopping for a new cell phone was not at the top of my personal priority list, but I certainly couldn't live without one. I didn't want my sister and her family to be bothered with my weird new job since they had their own business to run. And while my phone was not the most glamorous, it had served me well. I tossed the dead phone carcass back into the drawer and shut it. I would deal with this problem in the morning.

For good or ill, the problem was solved for me. That morning there was a package delivered to me by overnight shipping. Inside was a bright, shiny, new smartphone which was a new phenomenon at the time. This one looked similar to the iPhone but had a lot more bells and whistles. Big screen, lots of on-screen buttons, a user manual that was at least five times the thickness of the phone itself. GPS, Wi-Fi, Bluetooth, and whatever-G was the most recent at that time. Everything.

"Wow," said Lillith's husband, Dan, impressed. "Where did you get that?"

I looked at the box. There was no return address.

"Secret admirer?" asked Lilleth, teasing.

"Yeah, right," I snorted. "But I think I know who sent it."

"Oh, that rich guy who hired you," Dan filled in. "That's a secret admirer I wouldn't mind having." We all laughed at the comment.

"I guess when he couldn't get through on my old cell phone, he figured I needed a new one. And since he worked in the industry, of course it had to be the top-of-the-line model. Although I'm not sure I'm happy about it. He could have asked first."

"Probably a business expense for him," Dan suggested. "You get to take a lot of things in deductions when you have your own business. Most of this house wouldn't have been repaired if we hadn't been able to get something back on our taxes every year."

Lilleth sighed and rolled her eyes, looking remarkably like me when I did it. "No kidding," she agreed. "I love this house but there's always something that needs fixing."

"At least you guys are willing to put in the time and money. Your customers appreciate it because they keep coming back. And I really appreciate you taking me in on short notice."

Lilleth hugged me. "You're family. That's what family does. Now go charge up that new toy of yours and show us how it works."

I laughed and nodded as I climbed the stairs to my room. I shut the door once I was inside the room and threw the box on the bed.

"Arrogant a-hole!" I fumed.

"I'm sorry you don't appreciate the gift," came a voice from the phone.

I jumped a foot in surprise, but I recognized the voice. It was Cyrus Winston.

"How are you doing that? The phone is off."

"There's a two-way communication chip I put in so we can speak directly anytime, anywhere. The phone has a solar backup charge and is always on. One of my pet projects that isn't feasible for large production," he explained. "At least not yet."

"Isn't this a bit of overreacting to the fact my own phone was dead?" I questioned. "I said I would work with you, not for you. There's a difference."

"Yes, I understand the difference. But you must agree that you are new to the paranormal experience. There might be times when being able to communicate immediately is an advantage. Just because you can speak with ghosts doesn't mean that is all there is to being sensitive. There are other, more dangerous, elements out there."

Loony tunes, my rational mind told me. "Like?" I challenged.

"Your next assignment may involve one of these dangerous paranormal beings if my hunch is correct. How soon can you leave?"

"I only just got back," I complained. "Besides, I don't own a car."

"I can send…"

"No!" I nearly shouted. "I don't need any more gifts from you. I can get my own car, thank you very much. Just back off. I hate being micromanaged."

He huffed, annoyed. "Very well," he agreed. "Let me know when you plan to leave. I'll book an extended stay at the ship hotel. Be sure to try the Sunday Brunch, it's excellent." The voice cut off and I knew he was gone.

I wrapped the phone in a towel and put it in the drawer with my broken one. The ability to verbally communicate with me twenty-four seven seemed like an invasion of my privacy and had me seriously rethinking this business relationship. I hadn't had anyone looking over my shoulder for almost ten years and that's how I liked it. I wasn't a wet-behind-the-ears cub reporter who needed an editor monitoring my every step. Once I had proven myself, my investigations were completed on my own without anyone breathing down the back of my neck. And I had done a damn good job.

My irritation stayed with me all that day and into the next. It was still with me when I found a solution for getting a car. Finding the vehicle was a snap though, as usual, the price haggling proved to be difficult. And not in the way most people would imagine.

Lilleth and I were arguing in the garage over the hood of their extra car. The one I had used for my San Diego adventure.

"Take the car," Lilleth insisted.

"No," I refused. "Only if you let me pay you something for it."

"You're family…"

"But that doesn't absolve me from paying you something for this car," I interrupted. "You guys bought it and even though you don't use it much it's still worth something."

"But you don't have a steady job," she countered.

I bristled at the statement because it was mostly true. "But I do have money to pay you. And I have a sort of, very strange, part-time job."

"You can't count on this ghost hunting thing to last forever. And I think it's too stressful for you. Look at what almost happened in San Diego." She full-on in her big sister, protective mode.

Dan looked at both of us, stubborn as mules. He wisely kept out of the discussion, but I was sure they could have used the extra cash. Plus, they were losing money on the room I was using.

I turned my volume down and spoke more calmly than I felt. That bit about being out of a job had hurt. I was always proud of what I did for a living and having that taken away from me was a big adjustment. And she was right about the ghost hunting being dicey as a permanent gig.

"Look. Let me pay you two thousand dollars now and when I get paid again by Winston, another two thousand. That's better than you'd get for a trade-in and less than what I would pay at a dealer."

Lillith's mouth was stretched in a thin line, but finally she relaxed it and agreed, "Alright. Only because we really need to upgrade one of the bathrooms."

I saw Dan smile with delight from behind his wife and he gave me a thumbs up salute that Lilleth couldn't see. I nodded at them both. "Good. Let me go get my checkbook."

I hadn't owned a car since college because living in Chicago gave me decent public transportation and the advent of the internet helped keep me from running around to gather information. Most of my time researching was spent making phone calls, writing e-mails, and digging up dirt online.

Little did I know what awaited me as a car owner in the state of California.

Paperwork, paperwork, paperwork. Registration, a smog check, and mandatory insurance took another chunk out of my checking account to make me compliant with the state's regulations. It made me wonder why so many people owned cars in this state, then I remembered the number of no-toll freeways here compared to Illinois. The entire structure of California's transportation system was supported by those who used it, the car owners, through taxes and fees. I bit my lip and paid.

It was a few days after Winston's original summons when I finally was able to go forth and do ghost stuff for him and his web site. I was slightly unsettled by his hint that there were more things than ghosts out there; however, I put the feeling aside. I'd deal with it when the time came. That was my usual plan of action. I threw my well-worn duffel bag on the bed and began pulling shirts out of the drawer and taking clothes off the hangers in the closet. Rolling them up to conserve space, I started packing them into the duffel.

"Saddle-up, partner," I said to Styx. "We're on the move—again."

My feline friend hopped up onto the bed and dropped a toy mouse into the open duffel. I frowned for a moment; did he really understand what I meant? Then I could hear the tinkling of the little bell on the toy as the cat made a game of pushing it around the bottom of the bag trying to fish it out. Once he captured it, back it would go so he could do it all over again.

My eyes followed the waterfall of clothing as the contents of the bag were pushed aside in his eager search, slipping out of the duffel and landing in a crumpled pile on the floor. I sighed in resignation and wondered what had compelled me to keep this cat with me. Then I shook my head and smiled. He was worth the trouble.

CHAPTER 2

It was about a three-hour drive from Idyllwild to Long Beach.

According to Dan it was supposed to be two hours and some change. I also had printed a map to follow because our phones didn't talk to us back then. The family wished me well as I pulled out in my newly purchased car, heading down the mountain for my next adventure. Styx was curled up in my bag on the floor of the passenger side which I deemed to be a fairly safe spot for someone who couldn't wear a seatbelt.

By the time I reached my destination, I realized Dan had been optimistic. For the last hour of the trip, I was cursing loudly at the idiot drivers and praying that this hippy-dippy state would invest in some decent public transportation. Miles of freeway, multiple lanes going each way, and the number of cars on the road at any given time made for a harrowing trip for someone used to the L train in Chicago. Drivers cut in front of me on numerous occasions with little room to spare or changed lanes with no indication other than to move into the lane where I was currently driving, or to drive in what was supposed to be the fast lane at under the posted speed limit.

The bad part was my blood pressure was several points too high by the time I found the final freeway toward my journey's end. The worse part was I so stressed by the other drivers, I took a wrong exit and drove into the area across the bay from where I wanted to be. Sitting at a stoplight on top of a hill, I saw the ship clearly with no idea how to get across the water to the other side.

Thirty minutes of wrong turns and backtracking showed me a portion of Long Beach that was very beautiful, although almost any city near the ocean would fall into that category. It boasted not only a very busy port for cruise lines and container ships, but also a thriving oil industry, which surprised me as I really don't associate California as being an oil state, especially the seaside portion.

As I drove around a block to get back on the freeway and find the correct exit to where the Queen Mary was docked, I noticed political protestors marching around the convention center. This scene only added to my frustration, and I gripped the steering wheel tightly as a cramp passed through my gut. Here were people actively representing what I had done for so many years – questioning the status quo, refusing to take "no" for an answer, finding out why things were the way they were, and trying to make changes for the better. It had been a stressful, chaotic, and sometimes dangerous life, but I had loved every minute of it.

A wave of sadness washed over me as I watched them, rhythmically chanting, and holding their picket signs high. I had written about big things, important things, things that made a difference in people's lives. My audience may not have been nationwide, but it was a good swath of the

Midwest considering my paper's sphere of influence. What was I now? Now I was merely a hack who reported on ghosts for a bazillionaire with a thing for the paranormal. The audience was small, and the subject matter concerned only a few. It almost made me turn around and drive back to Idyllwild.

Almost.

I gritted my teeth and continued on, firmly willing my mind to put that part of my life behind me. I finally got back on the road and followed the signs to where Her Majesty, The Queen Mary, lay in her permanent berth. The sun sparkled on the water and reflected on the stark white of the ship's hull. I pushed my discontent aside and focused my thoughts on the job at hand.

I pulled a parking ticket from the machine at the entrance and made my way closer to the ship on the far side of the parking lot. Being mid-week and off season, I had my pick of parking stalls. Choosing one as close to the ship as I could without requiring a handicapped sticker, I took my duffel from the trunk then hoisted my bag/cat carrier over my shoulder and made my way towards the ship. The man at the booth asked if I was staying over and when I gave him my name, he confirmed that I had a reservation at the hotel for five days. Apparently, that was what Winston thought was an "extended stay." I hoped the ghosts were cooperative during this timeframe because I was pretty sure I didn't earn overtime.

I boarded the external elevators to the deck—not a floor but a deck, because this was a ship first and a hotel second— and pushed to button for the level where the check-in was located. However, in my irritated state, I pressed the wrong button.

Instead of the hotel lobby, I stepped onto the Promenade deck where the shops were located and the restoration was breathtaking. I was immediately swept up in the 1930s dedication to craftsmanship and attention to detail. I don't claim to be any kind of historian or interior designer, but even my cynical senses could appreciate the work that went into making this ship an artifact of a bygone age. Cautiously, I looked at my hands to make sure I was still solid and real and not in that weird time warp experience I had at the Whaley House. For a brief moment, it seemed like it could have been the same thing. Then a couple passing by in modern clothes with their attention captured by their cell phones broke the spell and reminded me I was still in the here and now.

As I stood there for a moment getting my bearings, I felt the stirring of ghostly things deep within the vessel as well as a distinct hint of something evil—a term I do not use lightly. In addition to the dark entity, I was surprised when there was a wave of familiarity that washed over me, which was strange because I'd never been there before. I shrugged it off and found some stairs that led me to the hotel counter. This deck was also beautiful, made of rich, polished woods with an art deco flair. There must have been at least five different types of wood used in the counter alone, ranging from almost blond to deep, dark brown. The overhead fluorescent lights reflected off the highly varnished surfaces. It was more than just a counter, it was a piece of art.

"Just yourself?" asked the lady with the plastic smile behind the counter as she looked up my reservation.

"Uh, yes. It's kind of a present to myself," I answered, half-smiling.

She nodded, not looking at me or really listening to the comment and took my information. "I see we have something that arrived ahead of you," she noted, handing me an envelope.

It was addressed to me via the ship/hotel but with no return address. I tore open one end and found a platinum American Express card with a note from my so-called boss.

Use this for expenses, the handwritten message stated.

"So, are you charging your room to the card you reserved it with?" asked the clerk with impeccable timing.

"Yes," I slid the card across to her. I hoped I didn't have to submit an expense report at the end of this little trip. I fleetingly wondered if psychological counseling for paranormal burnout would be covered under California's Workman's Compensation program. Probably not.

"Do you have a car in the parking lot?" she asked, typing away at her keyboard and hardly taking the time to notice me.

"Yes."

Clickety-clack went the keys as she entered more information. Then came the sound of the nearby printer. Still not making any eye contact, she reached below the counter to retrieve the paper it had spit out.

Plastic lady pushed the paper and my room key across the counter. "If you'll just sign here, you're all set. Your room is down this hallway on the right, you can't miss it." The words all came tumbling out in a rush and blended together.

Since no one was behind me, something stubborn made me stand there and not move. She had turned away and was busying herself with another task. When she turned back, the fake smile was back as she thought I was another guest to check in. Her face fell when she actually looked at me.

"Is something wrong?"

I shook my head. "No, I just wanted to see what color your eyes were," I replied cryptically. Then I grabbed my bags and left the counter, enjoying my triumph of rupturing her mechanical actions.

It always irritated me when jobs that required people skills were filled by people with little or none of those skills, or were not provided training to learn them. There is nothing wrong with showing respect for another human being and it costs nothing to offer it. Especially when that human being spends money that ultimately pays their wages.

Before heading to my room, I went back out on the deck and stopped at the Passenger Information Desk to see if I could get in on the midnight ghost tour of the ship. I was told that the tour was sold out for this evening, so I purchased a ticket for the following night. I was slightly shocked at the ghost tour price since it seemed high to me, but the cost didn't seem to deter other people. I recalled that great American tradition of charging for perceived value rather than actual value.

I knew for certain that I would see ghosts at some point during my stay, but I felt sorry for those who didn't have my sensitivity and were paying for the hope of seeing something spooky. I made a mental note that if I got tired of being Winston's lackey, I could do these types of gigs for a living. Paranormal was a hot topic at the time with books, television shows, and plenty of websites devoted to the subject. Making a living by promising the insubstantial to those who desperately wanted to believe was a profitable business plan for many. I immediately banished the thought. That wasn't me.

Noticing my disappointment that I couldn't get in on the paranormal tour, the man behind the counter suggested I take the Ghostly Legends Show. He said it covered a lot of the same things as the other one but was more spectacular. I glanced at him, confused by the use of the term, and bought a ticket since the times were plentiful. A historical tour was scheduled for later that afternoon after the ghostly one, but my tired body told me it would be too much for the first day especially after running the juggernaut of the drive from Idyllwild to here. The historical tours would have to wait until next day, but I added them to my purchase.

Having made good use of my benefactor's credit card to pay for the two ghost tours, I picked up my bags and headed towards my cabin. I got lost a couple of times because when someone tells you "You can't miss it," you know for a fact that you will do the exact opposite. However, the non-plastic and friendly staff soon had me pointed in the right direction. With the ship permanently berthed, it was hard to tell forward from aft since it wasn't moving.

When I opened the door to my cabin-room, I could only stand in the entryway and stare in wonder. Winston had booked a suite and it was absolutely gorgeous to behold. Gleaming wood paneling, classic nineteen thirties furniture, and art deco touches all around. The built-in tables and chests all had rounded edges, which made sense since the seas could get rough and throw people around the room. Much nicer to not hit yourself on a sharp, angled table corner. Modern amenities included a modern TV, docking stations for MP3 players, digital alarm clocks, modern bedding and blankets. But even with the 21st century items, the room still retained its 1930s glamor.

I could tell that this particular room had been recently refurbished. The carpeting had a new smell to it and the pattern was much too bright to be original. This was one of the higher priced First-Class cabins with a separate sitting area and large portholes that overlooked the water and gave a stunning view of all the restaurants and bars on the other side of the bay. Walking through to the bedroom, I was confronted with a king-sized bed that promised all the space I could take up with no one to care except Styx.

Speaking of Styx, he had managed to work his way out my bag on the bed and was stretching his cramped muscles. I stroked him along his back, and he nudged my hand with his head, purring. He jumped down and proceeded to inspect the room, peering into closets, sniffing the carpeting, batting open the door of the bathroom to investigate further. I removed a disposable cat box from my luggage and put it in the closet for him. I could close the door so housekeeping wouldn't find it and I was very grateful his messes were not that smelly. We had perfected our routine back in San Diego while investigating the Whaley House.

I pulled out my meager assortment of clothes, hung up the one nice outfit I brought for the brunch, and put my duffel away. At the desk I plugged in my laptop to get it charged, then stretched out on the bed to grab a quick nap before my ghost show. That stressful drive had left me exhausted, which made me congratulate myself for postponing the other tours. A slight shaking made me open my eyes to see that Styx had jumped up on the bed to join me, snuggling close. As I dropped off to sleep it occurred to me that he had made himself a permanent fixture in my life in such a short time.

I woke up in plenty of time for my show feeling refreshed. The touristy types were still aboard as I strolled around and took in the beauty of the ship, despite unrestricted kids darting around with clueless parents following. They had no concept of the majesty of this icon from another time in its hand-made splendor. I continually marveled at the time, money, and skilled craftsmanship used in the making of this vessel. In today's world people didn't really care about handmade items or paying for an artist's time and passion.

Without my feline partner, I lined up with the other ticket holders for the Ghostly Legends Show—which was well-named since it really was a show. It had little to do with the history of the ship or the ghosts and their stories. The entire thing was packaged like a cheap haunted house experience. The thing was so cheesy it should have been called Velveeta.

They presented a video in the waiting room which was supposed to explain the ghost legends. People drowning in the pools, the destruction of an escort ship during World War II, and an unfortunate crewman who was killed during a drill when the ship was brought to Long Beach. I had read about these incidents, but the flickering lights and piped-in scary sounds were distracting. Once the door opened, we followed our guide down a hallway with fake spider webs and black lights ending up at the First-Class pool.

The pool area was unrecognizable from my dream. The artistic touches could not be seen in the dim lighting, while the pool itself was filled with pipes used to create a fake mist or fog. Cords and wires littered the floor to power strobe lights and speakers. The actual beauty of the pool along with the ghosts weren't enough for modern audiences; the experience had to be "pumped up" with special effects. Hooray for Hollywood.

The group was on the upper walkway overlooking the pool, but it was so cramped I couldn't really see anything except for flashing lights interspersed with creepy sound effects. After the First-Class pool, we wound through several hallways and loaded into a service elevator, supposedly to descend into the bowels of the ship. We exited the elevator onto a platform and were told walk down a narrow catwalk.

Rumbling from hidden speakers and emergency sirens were sounds supposed to represent the time the Queen Mary struck another ship. Fake panels in the fake hull opened to let water pour in around us, as if they were really damaged.

Except for a tickling sensation of something that felt familiar to me, there was a complete lack of any ghostly presence which told me we were nowhere near the place where the Curacoa sailors drowned. Our guide's command to hurry was said with all the passion of a someone watching paint dry. The rest of the tour was a mockery of the events that led to the existence of the actual ghosts. Even crewman John Pedder, who was crushed by the watertight doors during a drill, was renamed Half-Hatch Harry because John Pedder didn't sound catchy enough.

Once the show was over, I sought the upper decks to clear my brain from the onslaught of stupid. I tried to cool my ire by reminding myself that the money made from the show helped to restore the ship. Both the historical and the cheesy had to live side-by-side in order to keep the ship open, I rationalized. Still, I felt sorry for the actual ghosts in those show areas who had to put up with it.

History isn't appreciated by everyone, especially school kids. Those of us who have lived several decades begin to appreciate history because we can personally recall events which happened during our lifetimes that eventually became history. Young people hadn't lived long enough to appreciate the time they were currently living through.

I leaned on the railing and enjoyed the breeze off the water, loving the scent of the ocean and the sound of water moving just outside of the ship's berth. There was no movement from The Queen, she was held firmly in her protected area of the bay. Not that seasickness was a problem for me. My family history was loaded with people who worked and lived on ships. Even as far back as the first of the MacIntyre Clan, a story I heard often from my grandfather. My Scottish pride had committed the story to memory.

As Grampa Mac explained, the Gaelic translation for MacIntyre is "son of a carpenter", but it was actually on a Norse galley that the first of my clan, Macarill, made his fame. He was nephew to Lord Somerled of the Western Isles, and he helped his uncle win the daughter of Olav the Red, Norse King of Mann, as his bride.

The story goes that Macarill bored holes in Olav's galley and filled them with tallow which is a wax rendered from fat. Then, Macarill made sure he accompanied the Norse king on his next voyage. When the heavy seas knocked out the tallow plugs, water threatened to sink to boat. After making Olav promise his daughter to Somerled, Macarill stoppered the holes with wooden plugs he had brought with him.

Tricky and clever. Also, a testament to how far we MacIntyre's will go to accomplish something. The memory of my grandfather telling that story made me feel warm and I smiled. Then I felt the tickling sensation again, the same that I had felt on the tour. I turned quickly to see if someone was behind me, feeling like I was being watched in some fashion. There was no one in the vicinity, not even annoying kids. Seagulls disturbed the quiet with their calls, but there was no human presence in my area. I shivered involuntarily.

"I need a drink," I declared to myself. "And probably some dinner as well." I pushed away from the railing in search of food, still uneasy from the sensation of being spied on.

I had not one but two drinks with my dinner. And it was a great dinner at the steakhouse on the ship. The advantage to living in the Midwest is having access to high quality beef, so I appreciated the fine cuts offered. I even saved some pieces for Styx who fully appreciated them. Well-fed and sleepy, we both sought the refuge of the bed. I slept soundly with no visions or ghostly dreams.

CHAPTER 3

Sleeping late is definitely my thing. DO NOT DISTURB signs are critical for someone like me, so I was extremely disturbed when there was knocking on my door at four in the morning. Groggily, I slid out from between the soft, comforting sheets, walked through the sitting room to the entryway, and opened the door. There was no one there. I peered right then left but saw no one in the hallway in either direction. Grumbling at having to make such a trek for nothing, I returned to the bed and dropped back into my slumber. If there was any more knocking, I didn't hear it.

Of course, the disadvantage of having a DO NOT DISTURB sign is oversleeping and almost being late when you have a ticket for a tour that starts in the morning. The adrenalin rush got me up, dressed, and prepped in record time as I ran out of the cabin, barely noticing that Styx also sped out the door before I closed it. I had about ten minutes to spare, so I bolted to the on-board Starbucks for coffee and a muffin. I am an expert at eating on the run thanks to my previous career. I was just brushing muffin crumbs off my shirt when I arrived at the meeting place for the history tour.

There was no one there except the guide.

"Are you here for the history tour?" he asked, hopefully.

"Yes," I answered, looking around for other people. "Am I it?"

He laughed. "I guess you are," he admitted. "If you want to take a later tour with more people you can come back this afternoon."

"No way," I replied. "I'd love a personalized tour. I'll probably have some unusual questions for you."

"Sounds great. Let's go." He gestured towards the lounge area where our tour began.

Compared to the cheesy show the previous day, this tour was fantastic. I could linger in the areas that interested me—which was almost everything—and I was able to ask lots of questions about the history of the ship, the building materials, the class separation, and more. I could tell my guide, Richard, enjoyed my questions and that he didn't often get a chance to answer in detail.

Most of the First-Class lounges were used for meeting space, wedding receptions, or other gatherings. We managed to sneak into the Queen's Salon while staff were setting up for a reception. As I looked around the majestic room with incredible decorative details, I became slightly dizzy as the ballroom was overlaid with an image of the room from the 1930s. Spectral passengers in evening wear crowded the place, while modern day waiters and other hotel staffers passed through them as they set up tables and chairs. I clutched a chair back to steady myself and with that little movement, the images from the past faded away.

Fortunately, Richard hadn't seen me stumble and we continued our tour. When he asked me what brought me to the Queen Mary, I told him I was researching the ship for an article on the paranormal, which was mostly the truth. He immediately added a couple of stops not normally on his tour. He showed me the most haunted room on the ship, cabin B-340, which had so much paranormal activity the hotel stopped renting it out. Even standing in front of the door gave me shivers and I declined his offer to go in. I didn't want to confront whatever was in there, and I felt it was much happier being left alone.

I asked about seeing the First-Class pool minus all the special effects. He took me to a back entrance where I could stand by the pool itself. The activity in this area was strong and even if I didn't see any spirits, I knew they were there; lots of them. I started to ask Richard a question but the noise of a door opening above us cut me off. We were forced to leave as the next Ghostly Legends group started to fill up the walkway above the pool. I was disappointed that I didn't have more time as I had once again felt that sensation of something familiar which kept popping up. Someone or something was watching me, not with evil intent but more out of curiosity. I consoled myself with the thought that my midnight excursion was coming up soon, and I would have more time to converse with the spirits there. Even in the brief moment I had in the pool area, I was touched by their presence. One even patted me on the back in a gesture I interpreted as welcoming.

The remainder of the tour was very straightforward with nothing more supernatural. At the end, I thanked Richard for his attention to my questions. I even took his email address with a promise to send him a link to the article.

"Have you been on the midnight tour?" he asked.

I shook my head. "Not yet. I'm going tonight though."

"Just a word of caution. Our lady who normally leads the tours is away and we have a new person filling in. I don't know what her background is, but hopefully she'll be as good."

"Thanks for the head's up," I replied. "I'm fairly sure I'll be satisfied with the tour, whomever is leading it." I smiled, knowing that would definitely be the case for me.

I made my way back to my cabin feeling good about all I had learned; discussing history with knowledgeable people always improved my outlook. As I approached the door, Styx detached himself from the shadows of a cross-section of hallway and waited while I opened it. He had an air of being very pleased with himself, entering the room with his tail high while I held the door open for him.

"Well, don't you look like the cat who ate the canary," I commented, then I paused for a moment when I realized what I had said. "You didn't eat any birds, I hope."

He just rubbed against my legs then made his way to bedroom.

"So, I'm thinking a late lunch and nap before the midnight tour. What do you think?" I asked him, in the doorway that separated the sitting room from the bedroom. I couldn't see him, but I heard the distinct sound of litter being moved around. He had ignored my chattering and gone straight to his litter box. I stepped back into the sitting room and left him do his business in private, falling into a chair at the desk. I pulled out my laptop and started it up, anxious to catch up with the 21st century.

I silently thanked Winston for making sure there was internet connection with the room. However, looking at the phone type plug I was supposed to use cautioned me that it might be a mixed blessing. This was still the early days of wireless so an actual plug guaranteed that there would be some type of connection to the world wide web.

I inserted the cord into my laptop and started it up, staring at the screen while I waited for my system to boot up and connect to the internet.

And I waited.

And waited.

And waited.

What would normally take about three to five minutes stretched out to almost fifteen. I should have guessed, given the age of the ship and the amount of money required to keep her afloat—or a-docked, or whatever it's called—that internet service would be a low priority. The speed was similar to the dial-up modems back in the early internet days. In a tortoise-like crawl that was painful to watch, the computer ran the browser program and downloaded my e-mail. With the swiftness of molasses going uphill in winter I was able to read and respond to the most important messages. It took every ounce of willpower I had not to throw the computer out the porthole.

After a couple of hours, I gave up, switched off the laptop, and headed out for my late lunch, early dinner. I was going to need some cool-down time prior to taking a nap before the midnight tour. I was hopeful this particular tour would give me the specific information I needed to solve whatever problem Cyrus Winston thought was on this ship.

As I exited the café after my meal, I knew I still wasn't tired enough to sleep because I continued to feel prickly and agitated. Fortunately, I had plenty of time to kill before my midnight tour, so I wandered through the small shops on the Promenade deck to kill time. The artsy-craftsy gift shop was cute, and the bookstore held my attention for at least an hour. Thinking I had seen all there was to see, I turned a corner to find the interior stairs and make my way back to the cabin. Instead of stairs, I was confronted by a store display that spoke to my very soul — a small, cramped shop dedicated to all things Scottish.

It was so small I almost passed it by, but the proud display of plaid in the window caught my eye. The shop may have been tiny, but it was packed to the brim with thistle emblems, flags, maps, and anything and everything Scottish. A poster for Highland Games recently held in the park area next to the ship explained this store's significance. But the showcase of it all was the wall of plaid at the back that I was totally unprepared for. Scarves and ties in almost every clan tartan imaginable.

My mind was instantly cleared of paranormal thoughts from that point on.

For those unlucky enough not to be Scottish, a tartan is the plaid fabric that each different Scottish clan wears. The colors and patterns are specific to each family. Clans can even have multiple colors and patterns of tartans, like ones for everyday wear or ones for fancy dress up occasions. The MacIntyre Clan has four tartans, Ancient, Weathered, Dress, and Hunting.

While my grandparents were proud Scots and had items with the clan tartan, they mostly assimilated into American culture. This made sense at the time because they wanted to strike their own path in their newly adopted country. And who needed all that wool when temperatures would get over

100 degrees in the summer? So, while our clan tartan was known to my family, it was never a big deal during my formative years.

But now, as an adult, looking at this piece of my heritage struck a chord within me. I was drawn to it. It represented something deeper than just myself or my immediate family. It represented hundreds of years and countless generations of people who identified with the name and pattern of this colored cloth. They lived and loved, fought and died, tethered to one another by a woolen strip of plaid.

I pulled the scarf from the rack and put it loosely around my neck. The weave was so fine it wasn't itchy at all, and it was lighter than I imagined it would be. It settled around me like woolen armor, ready to protect me from whatever the outside world could throw at me. Nana Mac would be pleased to hear about this when I got back to Idyllwild. Although her maiden name was Campbell, one of the largest and most influential Scottish clans, she was a proud MacIntyre. I was always surprised by her dedication to Grandpa Mac's family heritage over her own. The MacIntyres had been vassals of the Campbells hundreds of generations ago. But once she had married the man she loved, her fierce loyalty had been completely transferred to Clan MacIntyre.

I paused in my admiration. I wanted to have this scarf, but I really didn't have the cash to buy it. Wool is very expensive and wool fabric imported from Scotland was more than my budget would allow for. It was an unnecessary luxury I couldn't afford. Then I remembered Winston's credit card in my wallet. I could use that. Then I rejected the idea immediately. That card was for business not personal use.

But I really wanted it.

But it wasn't business-related.

But I really, really wanted it.

But it wasn't business-related.

But I really, really, really wanted it.

The debate in my head only lasted a fraction of a second. I bought the scarf with a vow to pay it back after this job. I placated my nagging conscious by thinking of it as a temporary loan. I considered the scarf a uniform of sorts. I declined a bag from the store proprietor and quickly pulled the tags off before settling the fabric around me. It felt right somehow, like it was part of me. My conscious finally shut up and I made my way back to my room to get that nap so I would be awake and alert for my next adventure.

And it definitely was an adventure.

At half-past eleven that night, Styx made a huge fuss to be let out. I was surprised at his insistence since he was usually very relaxed. He pawed at the door, looked up at me and cried quietly, then batted at the door again. I was already awake and getting my needed supplies for the after-hours visit to the ghosts on board.

"Okay, okay. I get the message," I said to him as I opened the door. He bolted down the hallway and disappeared around a corner. For a moment my heart sank thinking he didn't like our accommodations and was leaving me. I shook off the thought immediately. He would have made a stink a lot earlier if he didn't like being on the ship, so there must have been another reason for his demand. I shrugged and accepted it.

I arrived at the gathering place ten minutes before midnight with my fellow ghost hunters for our spooky tour of the ship. The gentleman at the check-in desk informed us that their regular psychic tour guide was away and there would be a substitute, exactly what I had been told by

Richard earlier that day. We all nodded in acknowledgement, and again, I was not too concerned about who was leading the tour as I was pretty sure I would get an up close and personal experience if any ghosts were about. The other phony ghost tour had soured my perception, and I hoped this one would be a better experience.

While standing around waiting for our guide, I noticed all were armed with flashlights as instructed. I was also carrying a notepad and pencil for jotting down anything interesting because old habits die hard, and I wasn't trained to take notes with a phone. My precautions were rewarded when the first thing our psychic-du-jour asked of us was to turn off our cell phones for the duration of the tour so we wouldn't be interrupted. There were a few grumbles, but everyone complied.

To be perfectly honest, the woman leading us scared me way more than any ghosts I was prepared to meet. She was a large woman who dressed in flimsy, lacey layers that only accentuated her size. While I am also a large woman, it wasn't her size that was the issue but her fashion sense. Also, her makeup looked like it was put on with a paint roller and I was sure we could see that neon blue eye shadow even with all the lights out. She took on the persona of a storyteller who was trying to frighten her audience which would have been amusing if she hadn't overplayed it so much.

My disdain for her act increased exponentially as I saw the shimmer of something out of the corner of my eye and felt that tingling sensation again. I looked over my left shoulder to see a tall, lanky young man with pants that barely covered his ankles, a collarless shirt, a jacket whose sleeves sat high on his wrists, and a cloth flat cap like British people wear. He smiled and winked at me. I knew he was a ghost and I nodded to him. He nodded back and we both turned our attention to the guide who was speaking to the assembled group.

"Oh, I have a feeling we have ghosts among us," she said in an overly dramatic voice. "I can feel the cold in this very spot. They must be here, very close to me."

Several people in the group oooh'd and ahhh'd, nodding in agreement.

The real ghost near me was the only one in the room I could sense, and we were at the back of the group, nowhere close to her. I glanced above her head and saw an air conditioning duct that was probably blowing cold air on her. I stifled my laugh with a cough.

"Sorry," I apologized quickly to the others. I saw the young man now beside me, laughing noiselessly. I wished I could do the same.

My unknown ghost friend stayed close to me during the tour. Being in my group of one, it was easy for me to hang back from the others and let the distance grow. I was extremely curious about this young man, and I wanted to talk to him. I finally got a chance when the group turned down a hallway and I found Styx waiting for me in a corridor near what used to be one of the boiler rooms. In retrofitting the ship into an attraction, almost all the boilers had been ripped out to make way for more storage and office space. I had read somewhere online that it was a condition set on the city of Long Beach to ensure that The Queen would never sail again. According to the brochure, only one boiler remained on the ship.

Now that we were alone, away from the group, the young man hovered above the floor with his feet disappearing into a hazy mist.

"Is that a moggie?" he asked in surprise, his voice a Scottish lilt very much like my grandparents.

"A what?" I struggled for a moment, processing his question.

"A moggie. A cat."

Styx turned to him, the neon lights of his green eyes shining bright.

"This is Styx," I introduced him. "I'm Shannon. Shannon MacIntyre."

His eyes widened in surprise. "Did you say MacIntyre?"

I nodded. For some reason there was a resonance from him. Something different from any of the other ghosts I had encountered, although that wasn't exactly a big number. There was that feeling of familiarity that had come over me ever since I had boarded.

"You've been following me, haven't you?" I stated. "Ever since I came on board."

He looked down, embarrassed. "Aye. I felt something pure tough with you when you set foot on the ship. I'm Andrew James Stewart MacIntyre," he added by way of apology. "I don't mostly leave my spot, but I been wanting to find you. Strange, isn't it."

"Yes," I agreed. I looked him over and felt some connection again. "Andrew MacIntyre," I said the name aloud while my mind sifted through information. "Why does that name sound familiar to me..."

Even as a child my passion for research had been evident when I was in school, especially subjects that stimulated me. Genealogy was always fun because it was so egocentric. I remember pouring over anything I could get my hands on at the time, which was limited due to the fact there was no internet, and I was at the mercy of what was kept at the local library.

One summer when my family was visiting the old homestead in Idyllwild, I asked Nana Mac about our roots. She brought out an old family Bible with Grandpa Mac's family tree; a nice tradition in the old days to keep a record of one's family in such a treasured volume. I looked at all the branches before me. Grandpa Mac's mother and father, himself, his sister, and a younger brother were listed in scratchy lettering, the ink turning brown with age. I had seen pictures of my great aunt but didn't know anything about a great uncle.

Of course, my childish mind was focused on finding my own name on the page, written in blue ink below that of my father, mother, and sister. In later years when the subject of family came up, I once asked my father about his uncle. He told me how Grandpa Mac's younger brother had died in a factory accident many years ago back in Scotland at the age of seventeen. Grandpa didn't like to talk about it, so that was all that we knew.

As I stared at this ghost of a young man carefully, I knew it had to be him. It fit the facts that I knew, and I could see some traces of resemblance to Grandpa Mac. And my instincts told me I was correct in my assumption.

"You're the younger brother of Ambrose MacIntyre," I said with a calmness that surprised me. "Ambrose is…well, was, my grandfather."

The ghost of the young Andrew MacIntyre appraised me up and down. "So, you're the granddaughter of my big brother?" He was partially in awe, especially since I was much older now than the age he was when he died.

"It's probably hard to imagine him as a grown man," I sympathized. "Or even an old man, which he was during my lifetime."

"Aye," he nodded. "He was a big strapping man when I left home to work at the shipyard." He shook his head, overwhelmed by the revelation. "I'll be. My grandniece standing here before my eyes."

I smiled sheepishly. I knew this was a pretty big event for both of us to comprehend. We just stood, examining each other for a few moments not sure what to say. He had composed his form so that he was as solid as I was, three dimensional and his feet firmly on the floor. The ability of ghosts to change their consistency always amazes me. I'm not sure if it's due to emotion or something they control, but they can appear very real—which is why people who have sightings swear they think the ghosts are real people.

Finally, I spoke, breaking the awkward silence. "I'm sorry I don't have any pictures of Ambrose with me or on my phone. Maybe I could show you some on my computer."

"Computer?" the word was foreign to him. "Do you mean the wee picture screens I see so many folk carrying around with them?"

"Yes, yes," I nodded enthusiastically.

Suddenly, I was very grateful that Andrew was born in the 20th century and could relate to movies and telephones. It was easier to grasp the concept of televisions, computers, and cell phones as the evolution of the things he was familiar with. I couldn't even begin to imagine trying to explain cars, computers, or cell phones to someone from an earlier century. The one hundred years of invention had begun before his birth in 1917 and was almost three-quarters of the way through when he died in 1934. Explaining new technology was helped by his frame of reference.

Our family reunion was halted by a voice coming from around the corner.

"Hello!" The psychic leading the tour appeared from the connecting hallway. "You there," she said, squinting those blue shaded eyelids to make me out in the dimness of the corridor. "You need to catch up with the group. No wandering off on your own." She made no comment about the ghost standing next to me.

"Coming," I answered. "I was trying to fix my flashlight. The batteries got disconnected." I shook it for emphasis and turned it on. "There. It's working now."

She huffed and went back the way she came, expecting me to follow.

"Hopefully I can see you later," I offered.

"Oh aye," he agreed. "I'm always here." He smiled widely at the joke and then faded from my view.

At least I know where my sense of humor comes from, I grinned.

The rest of the tour was fairly lackluster. I was familiar with most of the documented ghosts on The Queen, having done some research before I made the trip. I had seen a little bit of activity that the tour guide never referenced, but most of it fit into what I had already researched. Styx was a master of ninja skills, keeping to the shadows and out of view while he accompanied me on the remainder of the tour.

When the group reached the First-Class pool, I finally got a clear view of the departed people in the area, which had a strong paranormal vibe. I heard other spirits but didn't see them. I was aware that many researchers identified this location as a sort of vortex for activity. A little girl was giggling, something under the stairs made a growling sound, I could sense ghostly water in the pool and spectral swimmers leaving wet footprints behind them as they made their back to the changing rooms.

The group made the rounds of some other guest areas where I spotted activity in the hallways and rooms. None of the ghosts seemed particularly disturbed, with the exception of some mild irritation over the tour group, and they seemed quite at ease. There was no indication of the disturbance Winston had referred to. As I had predicted, I experienced plenty of paranormal activity during the tour, but our guide was forced to fabricate sightings to make her tour more interesting. Additional evidence that she was not as sensitive as she wanted everyone to believe.

After the tour, Styx and I made our way back to the room. I had just crossed the threshold into the sitting room when I found my knees shaking and my legs threatening to fail. A rush of strong emotion washed over me, and I quickly pulled out a chair at the desk to sit down, to keep myself from falling. Soon I was shaking all over.

"What the…?" I was at a loss for words. The tour hadn't been that strenuous, we walked at a pretty sedate pace to accommodate the number of people. Nothing strange had happened, at least nothing strange for me; everything about my life was strange these days compared to what it had been. The only discovery had been meeting my dead relative. Was that the cause?

It seemed to me unusual to have such a reaction since it had never occurred with the other ghosts I had encountered. As I sat at the desk, the shaking slowed and then finally stopped.

Maybe it has something to do with our relationship, I thought. It was kind of mind- bending to meet someone who died over seventy years ago but appeared younger than I currently was.

Suddenly, I was hit with exhaustion, like a train plowing into me. I glanced at the clock and saw it was two- thirty in the morning. Even with the nap before the tour, the emotional meet-up with my great-uncle combined with my still-recovering-from-a-heart-attack status made it clear that I was still not at my 100 percent activity level. Without bothering to get my nightclothes on, I put out the lovely DO NOT DISTURB sign, turned off the lights, dragged myself into the bedroom, and fell onto the bed. I pulled the comforter over me, dropping off to sleep instantly.

If I had known then that I had missed the very thing I was sent to discover, I would have found a way back later after the tour. As it was, I spent another restful night luxuriating in the over-sized bed. My mission was delayed, but I slept dreamlessly until noon and awoke refreshed.

Coffee first and foremost. I visited the little bakery café on the ship, sitting at one of the small tables. I overheard one of the ghost hunters from the tour at the table next to me talking about our adventure. The man was describing the tour to some people who had not attended. When his description turned to a very dark and creepy place in the bowels of the ship, I had to look up and listen. He recognized me.

"Hey, you're the one that got lost during the tour last night, aren't you?"

"Yeah," I nodded. "The battery in my flashlight died. Good thing the tour guide found me."

"Good thing you missed that stop," he shivered involuntarily. "I've been on lots of ghost hunts, but I've never encountered anything like that place. Dark. Creepy. It was like something wanted to suck you in; take over your very soul."

"Glad I missed it then," I responded sympathetically. The jury is still out on whether or not I even have a soul, I thought sarcastically to myself.

My World War Two tour wasn't until the late afternoon, so I spent my time wandering through the public areas of the ship, enjoying the flourishes of art tucked into nooks and crannies. Because I had already explored the shops inside, I was walking on the outside decks. As I passed a chained-off set of stairs that led to the lower levels, Styx—who had chosen to accompany me—squirmed frantically in my bag which was his signal to be let out. I discreetly complied when no one was looking.

He crept into the shadows, all but invisible. His whiskers twitched as he contemplated the steps leading down, almost as if he were debating whether or not to descend. Finally, he stepped gingerly on the first step.

"Don't use anything as a litterbox down there," I warned him. He gave me a reproachful stare with those deep green eyes as if disgusted I would even suggest such a thing. Then he swiftly ran down the stairs to wherever he was going.

The afternoon tour was very interesting. I was aware from the history tour that the ship had quite a legacy before she was retired. She began her life as a premier cruise ship breaking several speed records during her heyday in the 1930s. This tour focused on her role as a troop transport during World War Two. War broke out for Europe when she was at sea, steaming towards New York Harbor. Once she arrived, she was immediately retrofitted for wartime use. Painted a solid gray for camouflage, she was nicknamed the "Grey Ghost." Cabin furnishings were removed so that racks of bunks, some three and four layers high, could be installed in the cabins. During the height of the war even the swimming pools held bunks.

Once the Americans entered the war she was filled to the brim with soldiers, over sixteen thousand on one trip. It was also during this time that the greatest tragedy of her career nearly shut her down. To avoid detection by German submarines, ships would run in a zig-zag pattern. In the waters of Northern Ireland, the Queen had accidentally run over— or the nautical equivalent—her escort ship, the British light cruiser Curacoa. Due to it being wartime, the larger ship could not stop to rescue the survivors and.most of the crew downed.

According to our guide there was still speculation on what happened and why. One explanation was that the Queen was operating under specific wartime orders while the captain of the Curacoa was operating under standard maritime practices. Whatever the reason, over two hundred men died because the Queen would not stop to help. Hearing the actual story of the mishap made me even more irate over the pretend hull breech in the cheesy show.

After the tour I wandered to the aft of the ship to see the museum. While the upper floor had some great models and panels with the history of the Queen, I found my way to the engine room below and spent the majority of my time before dinner navigating the cramped spaces there. When I was alone without any other people nearby, I was given a first-hand account of the engines and boilers by my great uncle. He never appeared but his voice in my ear quietly recounted what each piece of equipment did to propel the ship. It was fascinating and I was almost sad when I had to leave this personalized narration to make it to my dinner reservation.

Tonight's dinner was seafood instead of steak, although I opted for a Caesar Salad with salmon instead of a big dinner plate. Even with just a salad the portions were large, and the clam chowder appetizer made for a filling meal.

Immediately following my dinner, I found a lounge chair on the deck and sprawled in it, watching an absolutely spectacular sunset. I didn't get to see a lot of sunrises and sunsets in my former job, so I appreciated the times when I could. A small burp escaped, disturbing the quiet around me; I was glad no one heard. My poor digestive track was overwhelmed by all the big meals I was eating, so I was grateful for the short timeframe my employer had imposed. If I continued like this for a week, I would undo all my previous weight loss. I made a silent promise to myself to be more calorie conscious during the rest of my stay.

As darkness closed in, I felt a presence next to me that coalesced into Andrew, finally showing himself after guiding me through the engine room. I preferred to call him by his first name and refused to think of him as an uncle because of his young age. It just felt weird calling a seventeen-year-old kid "uncle." Andrew was good enough; I called my other aunts and uncles by their first names as an adult.

"Styx wants you to come down to the Bosun's Locker—I mean the forward hull," he said quietly. "The door behind you is unlocked. You can snib it back up after you go through. Take the stairs all the way down." And with that he was gone.

I sat there momentarily translating his Scottish into my English. Styx wanted me to come to the forward hull using the door behind me and I needed to lock it once I was through. Okay, I got it. Then I bolted upright as the realization hit me.

The cat had commanded me to appear.

The cat.

Styx had apparently made his wishes known to Andrew who verbalized them to me.

The cat!

Actually, it really wasn't all that surprising. He never did act like a typical cat and his powers of communication were impressive.

But. The cat!

Granted I had had an inkling of his uniqueness since our first adventure in San Diego.

He's a cat!

I'm taking orders from a cat!

Sighing in resignation, I forced myself off the chair, slipped through the door—making sure to "snib it" as Andrew had instructed—found the stairwell, and made my way down. When I stepped onto the bottom landing, I was overwhelmed by a strong presence before me. It was pulling me forward and I could feel the darkness radiating from it before I even got close. With hesitant steps, I followed the compulsion but stopped in a doorway, willing myself not to go any further with a conscious effort.

This must be what that guy was talking about this morning, I thought. The presence was every bit as creepy and soul-sucking as the man on the ghost tour described. Even Andrew wouldn't go near it, he maintained his distance with me in the doorway. The room was empty except for a worn wooden chair.

The location was the section of the ship that had been damaged after hitting the Curacoa. The screams and shouts of downing sailors could be heard by those sensitive enough to hear, which included me. Their ghosts continued to beg for help, but no one could help them now. Only the heart-wrenching screams remained.

I allowed myself to be pulled into the room, stopping by the chair. There was a sensation of darkness, evil, aggression, and need that was almost overwhelming as it lay over calls from the lost souls. It was different. Ancient and powerful. I had never felt anything like it, although I acknowledged my experience was still very new. Hesitantly, I reached out and touched the metal panel before me.

Just as it had happened before in the Whaley House, I was transported back in time. The room around me, which had been silent in its berth, now vibrated with the pulse of the mighty engines and I could feel the rocking motion of a ship at sea. But however loud the engine sound, it was not enough to cover the screams of dying men on the other side.

Men in uniform surrounded me, they were real and solid. I brought my hand up to my face, but it was like the rest of me, invisible. Those around me projected feelings of intense anger and deep sorrow. All of them were frightened. A young man, not much older than Andrew, was huddled on the floor crying. Another soldier was muttering a prayer under his breath, asking for help from a higher authority, something the men in the room could not offer.

To my right, a man with sergeant's stripes was arguing with a superior.

"We can't leave them to die like this. It's inhuman." There was pain and anger in his voice. He was a frustrated as the rest.

The commanding officer was stone faced and his voice was not loud but forceful. "The ships' crew have their orders and we have ours. Their captain was expressly commanded not to stop due to enemy U-boats in these waters. This ship must maintain its present course and speed. Even slowing down would put the entire ship in danger. There's no point in dying before we even get to our destination."

"It's their own fault," an officer of the ship spoke up, disgust evident in his attitude. "If their captain had yielded as is required during wartime, this wouldn't have happened. Damned Royal Navy egotist." He was clearly looking to deflect any blame towards their ship for the terrible accident.

The man saying a prayer stopped and looked straight at the ranking officers, his eyes were steady as he held the other men with his gaze. He seemed to burn with an inner fire. It was almost as frightening as the screaming men who were drowning.

"It doesn't matter who is at fault," he said loudly, but with authority. "Those dead and dying men are blameless; they were merely following their orders." He looked around the room, making eye contact with each man there. Many couldn't face him and looked away.

"Something evil will come of this," he warned. "Those men are suffering, and their souls will not rest easy. The Devil will find a way to punish us for this transgression and wreak havoc on our world. The actions of both captains have cursed this entire ship." His voice rang with a conviction that stilled every voice in the room. The officer from the ship looked shaken, moved by the powerful statement.

"That's enough, Johnson," snapped the sergeant, sounding more afraid than angry. "Save your proselytizing for the battlefield." Although his voice wavered, the command was enough to break the hold of the young soldier.

"Hmph," was Johnson's reply as he returned to his prayers and said no more.

The death cries continued.

The scene started to fade out, but instead of returning to my time it was replaced with inky darkness. It was thick and cloying, causing me to choke. Mental, physical, and spiritual blackness closed in, enveloping me. Caught off-guard I couldn't fight back. I was sinking into it, helpless. I tried to claw my way through it, but everything was too heavy, like being sucked into a tar pit. The weight of it was crushing me. I gasped, trying to breathe.

Not only was it sticky and sucking the life from me, but it was also smelly. The putrid scent caused me to choke on bile as I struggled not to vomit, which would probably be impossible since I could use my lungs. I was drowning in this evil, foul-smelling muck which was preventing me from returning to my own time.

In my usual stubborn fashion, I fought back.

Let go of me, you stinky darkness! my mind screamed at it. Anger and rage boiled up inside me.

There was a split second of hesitancy then a sharp tug pulled at me, and I found myself lying on the floor on my back staring up at Styx who was sitting on top of me. His eyes were neon, but his entire body was fluffed out in fear and distress. His back was arched, and he hissed at me when our eyes met, but then he calmed down enough to reach out and gently tap my cheek with his paw. It seemed he had to reassure himself I was really alright. I stroked him along the back, smoothing down his fur. He nudged my hand when it neared his head.

"It's okay, buddy. I'm okay," I said in a cracked voice. He jumped off me as I sat up and clumsily stood up on shaky legs. I saw Andrew shuffling nervously in the doorway looking very frightened.

"Saints be praised, you're alright," he gasped. "I thought we lost you." The relief could be heard in his voice. He removed his cap to wipe his face even though there was no sweat.

I swallowed several times to get the words past my parched throat. "What the hell was that?" I finally squeaked to the ghost of my great-uncle.

"Something that doesn't belong here," was his solemn answer.

CHAPTER 4

Even while I tried to reassure him I was fine, Andrew insisted on following Styx and me back to the room to make sure I was okay. I didn't admit it to him, but I was glad for his company. It helped to have someone human—at least formerly human—to talk to about this case. Struggling out of the darkness had frightened me.

Once inside, I sat shakily on a chair in the sitting room. "That was the creepiest thing I've ever experienced," I admitted. "I've never seen, or felt, anything like that before."

Before he could answer, a different voice responded to my statement.

"I warned you there would be things not related to departed spirits," came a slightly muffled but still arrogant reply from my bag.

Andrew startled. "What is that?" he asked. "Another spirit?"

"No, just my boss," I replied with a frown as I pulled the phone out. I had forgotten Cyrus Winston had complete control of my communication device and now I was reminded again how much he controlled me.

"Is this what you meant by your warning?" I asked, placing it on the desk nearby. "A little more description would have helped," I added sourly.

"And how, exactly, would one describe pure evil, Miss… I mean, Shannon," he replied curtly. "It really isn't something that can be explained over the phone. But now that you have experienced it, you know better what it is." There was a slight pause before he added in an accusing tone, "And why has it taken you two days to finally confront this presence?"

"Send a complaint to the event management. I couldn't get a tour until last night," I snapped back. His arrogance annoyed me every time we communicated, and even though he was right about needing to experience the presence to understand it, I wasn't going to tell him that.

"But how do we fix it?" Andrew looked at me. "Those on the spirit plane are afraid of it, and it's getting stronger every day."

"A very good question that I'm afraid I don't have an answer for, Mister MacIntyre. That is something you will have to figure out for yourselves," Cyrus replied.

My mouth visibly dropped open. Partly because Mister Know-It-All didn't have a solution, partly because he was so polite to my great uncle, but mostly because he responded to Andrew's question.

"You heard Andrew?" I was stunned. Ghosts could actually be heard over this device?

As if reading my mind, he answered, "I told you I have sensitivities similar to yours. And this device is not your typical cell phone. But you already know that." He was smug again.

"So, what exactly is this thing that attacked me?" I asked.

"I believe it's demonic in origin, given the history of the location where it is emanating. Lost souls can be a doorway for things of an evil nature. I'm fairly certain this is an ancient entity but without knowing where it came from and what has caused it to appear at this moment, there is not much more I can deduce." The man sounded as if he were discussing his gardening techniques for all the emotion he didn't display.

"Demons. Seriously?" Ghosts were bad enough, but this was a higher level of crazy. I could barely wrap my mind around it and my natural cynicism took over.

"I'm very serious," he replied. "You'll need to put all your investigative skills towards finding a way to defeat this entity. My site and others should be helpful to you."

"So that's it, then? Just a 'good luck, chief' and off we go. What use are you then?" my great-uncle rebuked him. "A voice over a radio can't be no help. Be off with you then, and let Shannon and me figure this out."

Andrew's scorn was clear, and I wanted to hug him for the support. He basically told Winston to "piss off" since he couldn't help and the two of us would solve it. The sentiment was something I would have wanted to say to him but didn't because the guy was paying me fairly well for my time. I just smiled at Andrew in appreciation.

In indomitable Winston fashion, however, he was unaffected by Andrew's retort. "Whatever help you can lend Shannon is appreciated, Mister MacIntyre. Be sure to report to me when you've finished your research, Shannon. I may be able to add some extra information from personal experience." It was business-like and unemotional. But I still gave Andrew props for his comment.

"Will do," I replied, ending the call and tossing the phone back into my bag.

"Well, he's a gommy bawbag, isn't he," my ghost-uncle commented.

"Yeah, but since he pays me, I can't say so. I'm sure you had bosses who were the same way." I had no idea what a 'gommy bawbag' was, but I figured it was the same as asshat or jerkwad which was the modern American equivalent.

"Aye. I did. But I only had the one and I didn't last too long on that job," he smiled with a twinkle in his eye.

I stared at him blankly for a moment then got it and chuckled at his grim humor. He had been killed on his first job. Maybe he was lucky in that respect because he didn't have to spend a lifetime working for people less smart than he was.

"Here," I grabbed my laptop. "Let me show you some pictures of your brother and the rest of this family. We can do some catching up before working on our demon problem."

We sat together for almost an hour as I brought up the pictures I had transferred to the computer several years ago. I had scanned a lot of old photos that were in danger of disintegrating to help preserve them and since my computer is my extra limb that I can't do without, all files were automatically stored on it as I made upgrades through the years.

Andrew was in a trance looking at the evolution of the family he never met. Many of the pictures were black and white, grainy, and scratched, but he picked out his siblings instantly. He watched his older brother as he fought in the Second World War, married the woman he loved, moved to the United States, and raised a family. He was especially appreciative of the big house in Idyllwild.

"Nana Mac … I mean Audrey, is still there in spirit form," I told him. "She's the one who first came to me after I found out I had this gift."

"Did she?" he said with a trace of awe. "Fancy that." He looked up from the computer and stared at me. "I'd best be going back to my engines. You look a fright, lass, better get some sleep." He patted my hand which felt like a soft breeze flowing over my skin.

I nodded, feeling heavy and weary after my encounter with that soul-sucking darkness. I barely noticed him dissipate as I made my way to the bathroom to get ready to go to sleep. Styx stood guard at the foot of the bed until I finally crawled in and turned out the bedside lamp. We both snuggled down and my last fleeting thought before I drifted off was that I must indeed have a soul since the presence affected me like everyone else.

Good to know.

The next morning, I took my coffee on the deck with some fruit for breakfast. As I sat at a table and stared out over the water my mind sifted through my encounter last night with this evil that was haunting the ship. Questions littered my brain.

Where did it come from?

How did it get here?

Why had it only just appeared now and not years ago when the ship was first brought to Long Beach?

A journalist lives on questions and the hunt for answers. And sometimes the answers bring even more questions. To paraphrase the great Sherlock Holmes, the game was always afoot.

I was lost in thought when a small voice right next to me interrupted my musings.

"I like your cat," a little girl said to me with a large smile, pointing at my chair.

"Oh?" Startled, I looked around and saw Styx sitting placidly underneath my seat. He was totally and completely unperturbed about being seen. Why was he out during the day? "Thanks," I answered lamely.

A woman—I assumed the child's mother—stepped up hurriedly and took the girl's arm.

"I'm so sorry," she apologized. "She has a very vivid imagination." Then to the child she said, "Honey, there are no cats on the ship. It's not allowed. You're just pretending to see a cat." She started to walk away with the child in tow.

"But mommy," the girl protested. "I can see it."

"It's okay," I called after them. "She's fine." Inwardly I cringed as the mother berated the child for her vivid "imagination." She was only seeing what a certain sub-set of the population could see and feel. I completely sympathized with the little girl's plight. Some people never believed what others could see. I knew that from experience.

"Poor child," came a voice to my left. I swung my head around and saw an older black woman with a slight Southern drawl settling into the chair beside me. "Since when is having a vivid imagination a bad thing?"

I shrugged. "Insecure parenting. They can't handle their kids being 'different' in any sort of way, I guess."

"Do you have children?"

I laughed; the idea was so absurd. "No, I've been a workaholic most of my life. And I'd make a lousy parent."

The woman smiled at me. "It's a smart person who understands they don't have what it takes for one of the toughest jobs in the world. Nothing to be ashamed of."

"Are you staying on the ship?" I asked casually, ready to change the subject away from families and children.

She sipped from her cardboard coffee cup then shook her head. "No, I'm here with friends for the day but I don't want to go on the haunted house tour. I'd rather hear the real history than listen to something made-up."

"Good choice," I agreed. "It's pretty cheesy and there are plenty of real ghosts on board without having to make up new ones."

"Amen to that." She sat up and extended her right hand towards me. "I'm sorry, I neglected to introduce myself. I'm Luvenia. Luvenia Maxwell."

I pressed my hand into hers. "Pleased to meet you. I'm Shannon MacIntyre."

"That's a beautiful scarf," she said.

"Thank you. I bought it in the Scottish shop back there. It's my family plaid. MacIntyre."

"Oh my. That must be very old."

"Ancient," I replied.

"It's good to have a connection to your ancestry."

"Have you traced yours?" I thought it was an innocent question. I was very wrong.

"Well, people like me can only get so far. Almost all roads end at a plantation somewhere," she smiled sadly.

I felt my cheeks flush with embarrassment. "I'm sorry. That was rude …"

"No need to apologize, sugar," her eyes were kind. "Can't change the past. We just need to make the future better for everyone."

I nodded vigorously. "I definitely agree."

She moved her chair back and stood up. "I see my friends are here. Very nice talking with you."

I looked up at her with a smile. "You, too."

"And that is a nice cat you have there," she added before walking off.

Before I could respond she was out of earshot. I bent over to look under my chair and saw Styx lying there, legs tucked under him looking like a black loaf of bread.

"What is it with you anyways? Do you pick and choose when to be visible?" The mystery of him not appearing on the security video from our San Diego gig still baffled me. However, some things cannot be investigated, with cats being at the top of the list.

Styx just looked up at me with those huge, green eyes.

"At least we know she wasn't a ghost," I surmised.

There was nothing strange going on at the moment, not counting the demonic presence on the ship that wanted to take over everything. Nope, nothing strange at all. And I had the rest of the day to do research before venturing down to confront the darkness again. Or The Darkness, as I had been calling it. The title fit all too well.

After about five minutes of relaxing, I felt the prod of a paw underneath me and then a flash of black as Styx made tracks out from under the chair and around the corner. I got the feeling I should follow, so I stood up and walked as casually as I could in his footsteps. I don't know why I chose to follow him, other than that seemed to be what he wanted.

Another chained-off stairwell greeted me, with the chain dangling off its hook. Someone or something was making me welcome in the restricted areas of the ship, and I certainly couldn't resist the invitation. I slipped into the shadows, refastened the chain, and made my way down the steps. Soon I found myself in the First-Class pool area again but this time I was surrounded by almost all the ghosts on the ship.

I was surprised by the appearance of all the spirits at one time in a location that was frequently visited by the cheesy tour. I shot nervous glances to the upper walkway, afraid that I would be discovered standing in the middle of the area all alone; at least that is what it would have looked like to the tour group.

"It's alright," said Andrew, guessing the reason for my paranoia. "One of the guides didn't show, so we have time between tours."

I nodded, visibly relieved.

"Andrew says you're here to help," a lady in a 1930s swimsuit stated.

"Can you really get rid of that evil?" asked a young man in worker's overalls. I recognized him from the actual ghost tour—John Pedder, who had been crushed by a water-tight door during a drill in the 1960s. I withheld my impulse to ask his opinion on the Half-Hatch Harry moniker.

A young girl, who I later was introduced to as Jackie, was clutching her teddy bear and looking at me with her ghostly eyes pleading.

"Please, make it stop," she said quietly. A woman in white, who I had noticed in the Observation Lounge the day before, put a hand on the child's shoulder in a comforting gesture.

The sheer variety of people from so many different eras was mind-boggling. In addition to the 1930s swimmer, Pedder, the girl, and the woman in white were Ship's Officer William Stark who mistakenly poisoned himself when the liquid in a gin bottle was actually tetrachloride, a few soldiers, another woman in a 1960s swimsuit, and others who were not as distinct.

"Yes," I said, more confident than I actually felt. "I've been sent to help, but I'm still trying to figure out what this thing is. Does anyone know when it started?"

"Not that long ago," the woman ghost in 1930s swimwear answered. "When Mister Johnson stopped coming."

"Yeah, that's right," agreed Pedder. "It was shortly after he passed when that area become … infected." He shrugged not knowing what else to call it.

"Mister Johnson?" I asked, puzzled.

"Yes," the woman swimmer replied. "He came every day for years and years. He always visited that part of the ship and said a prayer or made some sort of dedication. He didn't start coming until after we had been docked here for a few months. But once he started, he never stopped."

"Oh, I remember him," added Andrew. "I would see him in the Bosun's Locker whenever I was in that section. But that wasn't often since I like to be with my boilers. In fact, I've seen more of the ship these past couple of days with you, Shannon, than I have for the last seventy years."

"Is that a compliment or a complaint?" I asked quietly, raising an eyebrow at him.

He smiled at me. "Ach, neither one. Just an observation."

I turned back to the woman in a swimsuit from the 1930s. "When was the last time you saw Mister Johnson?"

She smiled slightly. "It's hard to tell time here. From my view, everything is always the way it was and sometimes time just stands still. Maybe the purser can tell you, everyone on board knew Mister Johnson. He was a war hero."

Her last sentence clicked, and I recalled the man praying and foretelling dire consequences from the accident as I had seen in my vision. Johnson was such a common last name, but he did predict something would happen when all those men drowned. Did he really follow this ship to her home here in Long Beach? It seemed improbable ... but so was talking to ghosts and I did that every day.

I noticed two other children appear next to the young girl. They seemed protective of her. Even as spirits, I was struck by the fear in their eyes and in a rare moment of sentimentality, I saw my niece and nephew in them. I kneeled down to be on their level.

"I'll do everything I can to make it go away," I assured them. "I promise."

I turned back to my well-informed swimmer. "So, is this purser a physical one or a spiritual one?"

She laughed. "He works in the Information Booth on the Promenade Deck."

"Okay, thanks," I replied, hoping the note of relief didn't show in my voice. Talking to ghosts for a long period of time can be wearing.

Later that day I went in search of anything I could find about out Mister Johnson. The purser didn't exist at all, I found out. I believe the woman was remembering a person from her era when the ship was still a cruise ship. So, I asked at the Information Desk.

The Information Desk referred me to the Hotel Desk. The Hotel Desk referred me to the Information Booth outside of the ship, the Information Booth referred me to the Exhibit Hall, the area I had quickly bypassed the previous day on my way to the engine room.

Finally, I found someone who knew about the mysterious, and not quite well-remembered, Mister Johnson.

"I can't tell you much about him," the docent told me. "But his grandson is a volunteer. He's working over there in the display area today. His name's Brian."

"Okay, thanks," I replied.

In the display room, I quickly found Brian. Nametags are such helpful things.

"I'm sorry if this sounds weird," I prefaced my opening line. "But I think our grandfathers were on this ship at the same time during the war."

"What was his name?" he asked. He was brown haired and brown eyed with a natural tan of someone who liked to be outdoors. Brian looked younger than me by about ten years or so, but given my general poor health anyone under eighty probably looked better. I rattled off a name I had read on a list of American troops from an earlier tour, mentally crossing my fingers that it wasn't someone who lived in California. I didn't want it to be a person he might know from the area.

"Oh yeah, they were part of the Twenty-Ninth Infantry Division. Is he still alive?"

I shook my head. "We lost him a long time ago. He was only in his mid-seventies."

The sadness in my voice was real because it was my own grandfather I was thinking about.

He never sailed on the Queen Mary as he was a Scottish native, but he was a proud member of the 52nd Lowland Division.

"I'm sorry," Brian sympathized. "I just recently lost my grandfather and I really miss him. We both worked here as volunteers. He really loved this ship. Even when he couldn't drive anymore, he insisted on visiting at least once a week. We had some really good times together. I guess that's why I continue to stay on without him."

"Wow!" I put on my amazed face. "That's some dedication. I would think this place would have terrible memories of the war for him. I saw the display below us and those guys were really packed in here like sardines. Worse."

He smiled. "I thought so too, especially since the accident with the Curacoa happened when he was on board. A lot of the soldiers were more upset by that incident than what they saw during the war. But I think Gramps wanted to do something for the ship to protect the memories of those who died in the accident. And he was genuinely attached to the Queen. I think he felt it was his duty to continue to visit and to remind people that the horrors of war don't always happen on a battlefield.

"He was also really religious and wanted to pray for the souls lost. Towards the end of his life, he got a little demented and insisted that demons were invading the ship. You know how old people can be sometimes when they 'lose it'."

I nodded. "Yes, my grandfather was that way right before he died. He wasn't as religious, but he held on to his beliefs during those years. Heading into a war would make anyone religious, I think."

Sorry, Grandpa Mac, I silently thought. The man was as sharp as a tack up to the day he died. I didn't mean to tell lies about him, but I wanted to gain Brian's confidence.

He laughed and glanced at his watch. "Hey, it's time for my break. Do you mind if we continue this outside? They don't allow smoking on the ship." He pulled out a pack of cigarettes from a leg pocket on his cargo pants.

Oh shit. I dug very, very deep to find the strength to say "Sure, no problem."

"You don't mind, do you?"

"No," I lied again. "No, not at all." What was one more lie added to the ones I had already told.

Out in the smoking area of the parking lot, I stayed upwind of the smoke. It helped — a little. But only a little.

"Sorry about this," he gestured with his cigarette. "I know I need to quit."

"I understand. I just recently quit myself," I confessed.

"And you willingly came out here with me?" he was stunned. "Damn."

"It's easier to quit out here with all the regulations against smoking. I'm from Chicago where a lot more people smoke. Sometimes I think we do it just to stay warm in the winter."

He laughed at my joke. "Well smoking wasn't the only reason I came out here. Even though I volunteer on the ship, I'm also part of a group of historical preservationists who aren't happy with the way the ship is being managed."

Oh boy, controversy. The journalist in me loved these confessions. "Oh?" I encouraged.

"Please don't let me bore you if you're not into…"

"No. No," I stopped him. "I'm a huge history buff."

Mostly true. Especially if it revealed any tidbits I could use for my current assignment.

He blew out the smoke in his lungs and started in. "As much as management has done a great job restoring the cabins, they have almost completely destroyed the engine rooms. They should have been preserved as part of the ship's legacy. Instead, they've been almost completely torn out to make way for office space. Such a waste." He shook his head.

"But one of the tour guides told me they had to remove the boilers to ensure the ship would never sail again. I thought that was a condition of the city acquiring her," I pointed out.

"It was," he agreed. "But they didn't have to remove all of them. There were twenty-four Yarrow boilers in four rooms. Removing just one room would have ensured the ship would never sail."

"Isn't there still one on board?"

"One out of twenty-four doesn't even begin to show how incredibly this ship was engineered. It was a masterpiece of technology for its time. They should have left one entire boiler room to give people an idea of how amazing it was."

"Were they really that special? Today's tourist would find it pretty outdated machinery. Not nearly as interesting as ghosts."

He shook his head. "That's what we hear all the time. They were old, they don't count for anything. The problem is we don't know that for sure because there isn't anything that can be used to show how incredible the boiler system was. Did you see the chart about the boilers on one of the tours?"

"I found it on my own. Kind of hard to read since it's in a dark area. Actually, the whole room was dark."

"Exactly. Management gives absolutely no recognition to the system that powered the ship. See, the ship's story is more than just a cruise ship or troop carrier. The engineering of the boilers was way ahead of its time, especially during the thirties. The system helped the Queen maintain her reputation as the fastest ocean liner. She held the Blue Riband accolade for the fastest cruise ship from 1938 to 1952. That was due to the magnificent engines that today's generations will never know about. Millions of dollars have been spent to refurbish the cabins but the thing that made this ship truly great was stripped away. Students of engineering and even those who love history would be fascinated to see a complete boiler room. Why can't that part of the ship be preserved?"

"Because it doesn't make money," I replied. My cynicism came from an honest place. I had spent years among those in power and I knew about their obsession with finding any and all ways to increase their power, and that was mostly through money. "Money talks, history walks. People will pay to see, or not see, ghosts. The general public isn't interested in old boilers. Nothing mysterious about that scenario."

He frowned at my comment. "It's still wrong."

I knew exactly how he felt. "Oh, I agree. But until the world decides to make a serious attitude adjustment, nothing will change. I spent years as a reporter trying to find out the truth; but truth and fairness just can't compete with power and money."

He shrugged, accepting the statement and, thankfully, put his cigarette out.

"Did your grandfather become a volunteer because of the preservation?" I asked, wanting to get back on the original subject in my quest for information.

"No, although he agreed it was wrong to strip the engine rooms. He said it was his duty to visit the place on the ship where they heard the Curacoa sailors downing."

"The escort boat that was wrecked during the war?"

"Yes. You've been on the ghost tour?"

I nodded. "Both the cheesy Ghostly Legends and the midnight paranormal one. The paranormal one was interesting," I admitted.

"I don't doubt it was tragic for everyone involved, but it hit Gramps really hard for some reason. He made sure he was here at least once a week, rain or shine. He used to bring me when I was little, then I brought him when he couldn't drive anymore."

"Did you work in the same area?"

"No. He spent most of his volunteer time on deck telling his stories about the Queen during the war. I'm usually where you found me, in the display area."

"Oh. I was under the impression he worked below decks, from what someone told me."

That wasn't untrue. A ghost is a someone, just not a living someone.

"When he wasn't 'on display' he liked to go down to the area he was assigned during the war. I guessed he was reliving the old days down there. No one ever disturbed him; we all gave him is privacy."

"Wow. This ship must have been pretty important to him. All my grandfather ever talked about was that it was really cramped on here and he was glad to get off. Most of his stories were about fighting in the war." This also wasn't a complete lie because Grandpa Mac was on a crowded troop carrier, but only to cross the English Channel to France.

"It was very important to him. He got really agitated when he went into the hospital before he died. He was practically ranting about devils and demons. He even made me promise to get a priest out to the ship at least once a week to do a blessing. He really lost it at the end." A pained look crossed his face as he remembered.

"I'm sorry," was all I could offer. I could tell he was still feeling the loss.

He looked at his watch. "Guess I'd better head back." He started across the parking lot to the ship while I stayed where I was, denying to myself it was just to inhale the last bits of smoke from his cigarette. Suddenly he stopped and turned. "So how did you quit smoking?" he called back.

"Cold turkey. It's hard, but it works."

He nodded. "I think I might try it. I know Gramps quit after the incident here. Scared him that much."

"Thanks for the chat," I said, waving at him.

Your Gramps was scared by that thing for the rest of his life, I thought. And he certainly didn't "lose it" when he died. It's just that no one living understood his request. How could they?

Styx was lounging in the middle of the bed when I returned to the room, which surprised me because he had left the pool area with me but went off on his own as I did my scavenger hunt to find out about Mister Johnson. I knew there was no way he could get back in by himself. Unless teleportation was a trick of his I hadn't seen yet.

"How did you get back in?" I asked.

"I opened the door for him," supplied Andrew, appearing beside the bed. "But I made sure to snib the door again. Was that alright?"

"Sure, that's fine. I figured he just walked through the walls like you."

My great-uncle laughed. "Ah, you're dafty. He's not a ghost."

Well, that was one theory about Styx disproved. But I had plenty of others. I also found that my ear was getting better at understanding his accent. Apparently, Grandpa Mac lost a lot of his when he became an American citizen.

"How is it downstairs?" I asked.

"Bad," he replied grimly. "And getting worse. The night tours have been stopped because a woman was almost taken by that evil thing."

"What?" I had heard nothing about it.

"Aye. She had fit of madness after the tour," he shook his head sadly.

I thought I had overheard someone saying something about a passenger that had an epileptic fit recently. It fit if they were sensitive to that evil entity. I nodded.

"But is there nothing you can do about the evil?" His eyes were pleading.

"I don't even know what it is, much less how to stop it," I said with some exasperation. Cyrus Winston hasn't been much help for any of this. "I could recommend an exorcism to the people who run the ship, but that would cause them to throw me off for being a lunatic."

"Aye. You do have a difficulty with one foot in each world."

His comment struck me as entirely accurate. Is that how it's described? I wondered. Interesting. Better than "one foot in the grave," I guess.

I plumped the pillows to lean back against the headboard and settled myself next to the sleeping cat. He barely stirred other than to twitch his tail, acknowledging my presence. Andrew sat/hovered at the foot of the bed, reminding me of my first encounter with Nana Mac.

My nostrils caught the scent of something, and it smelled fishy—literally. I leaned closer to Styx's head and took a whiff.

"Where did he get fish?" I demanded from the sheepish-looking ghost.

He grinned showing beautiful white, even teeth, a hallmark of my family. We are an orthodontist's bane; braces are an unknown thing to us.

"Fair clever, that one. He found the room where they store the food for the kitchens and helped hisself. I told him not to have a go again because he could get caught."

I looked down at the sleeping cat. His body never moved but his pink tongue licked his lips in a gesture of satisfaction.

"Don't make it a habit while we're here," I warned him.

The tail twitched again.

"Did you find out anything about Mister Johnson?" Andrew asked.

I told him about my conversation with Brian Johnson, including his dismay about the boilers being torn down. Andrew nodded enthusiastically.

"Aye, it was a shameful thing they did. All the boiler rooms acted in perfect harmony with each other. It was a thing of beauty to behold and there's been nothing like it since." There was sorrow in his tone.

Andrew's love of machinery was probably a big factor in why my own father was a mechanical engineer. There must have been a genetic component. It made sense because I was also the techie person in the family and I loved new gadgets, especially my computer. Thinking about three generations of technology lovers, I felt an even stronger connection to my ghostly great-uncle.

CHAPTER 5

With no late-night ghost-hunting tours, the ship was calm and quiet. I heard people talking at dinner about a woman who had had a seizure during the previous night's ghost tour and, since the resident psychic was still absent, management decided to suspend the midnight tours. That would make my own prowling much easier.

Of course, the ghosts themselves could care less what time it was. They did what they wanted, when they wanted, whether or not they had an audience. They didn't care if you could see them or not, although some did appreciate having my presence, especially the little girl Jackie.

She sat next to me at the edge of the now-empty First-Class pool, our feet dangling into the space where the water used to be. She reminded me so much of my niece, I playfully "splashed" some water on her. She giggled and scampered away to get out of my reach. I couldn't help but smile, kids were kids no matter what era they came from.

The ship creaked ever so slightly as metal adjusted from the heat of the day to the chill of the night. The LED lamp I had brought lit the area around me, but outside the light the darkness and shadows closed in.

Darkness has never bothered me, and I actually enjoy the quiet. It was also refreshing to be away from people for a while. Living people that is. Even though I spent most of my adult life in a big city, surrounded by people, interacting with people, gathering news for people, I still found being alone in the dark soothing. Although, technically, I wasn't really alone.

A couple of ghosts in the pool area were enjoying themselves with a swim. I could hear the sounds of splashing and could almost feel water moving around my dangling feet. I tried to imagine how beautiful this was when the ship was still a cruise liner. What was left of the decorative tiles made interesting images in the wall across from me. Above me were windows that would let the daylight stream in. Walkways above allowed other passengers to watch the pool area and were probably much less crowded when the ship was still in service since there wasn't a tour group coming through every ten minutes or so. Such a different time from ours where craftsmanship and quality were prized; not the throw-away society we had become.

The sound of wet footfalls brought me out of my reverie. The ghost of the drowned woman from the 1930s sat beside me, toweling her hair. She had been very attractive at the time of her death.

"I usually swim longer but it's too scary with that evil darkness around," she explained. "I don't know what we'll do if it continues to expand. I wish Mister Johnson had stayed and not gone beyond."

Styx wandered over into the light and sat between us, his eyes neon green. I stroked his head for my own comfort.

"Mister Johnson only held it at bay," I responded. "He didn't know how or didn't have a chance to get rid of it."

"Do you know how to get rid of it?"

I shook my head sadly. "No. But I'm working on it." I thought of the woman who had had the seizure on the tour. I needed to make it safe for the living as well as the spirits.

Both of us stopped to watch a woman in a 1930s bathing suit step up onto the diving board high above the pool. She launched from the edge and made a perfect swan dive into the non-existent water with a splash.

"Well, back to the dressing room to change," said my ghost companion, rising. She paused for a moment then leaned down to touch my shoulder. I could feel the cold through my shirt. "You'll come up with something, we know you will. Andrew has great faith in you." She turned and walked away leaving wet footprints behind her.

"I'm glad one of us does," I mumbled.

Later on, I leaned in the doorway of the room where the evil thing lay. I knew not to touch it, but even without contact I could feel that it was stronger. And getting stronger. The room was not just cool, it was cold. I could almost see ice crystals forming on the hull panels.

Does that mean Hell is really freezing over? I thought fleetingly.

The ghosts called it evil. Andrew believed it didn't belong here. Brian Johnson said his grandfather talked of devils and demons. A tourist had gone into an epileptic fit. My own encounter had been something very different from anything I had experienced so far. This was something completely beyond the spiritual plane.

Andrew materialized beside me. "Can you feel it?" he asked.

"Yes," I answered, seeing my breath form into mist from the cold. Much colder than a paranormal type of cold.

"Have you been able to find out anything?"

I shook my head. "I'll have to get off the ship so I can do research with my computer. The internet access here is slow and takes too long."

Andrew shook his head. "Beg pardon? I don't understand any of that."

Ugh. How did even begin to explain? "Remember when I showed you my small movie screen and we looked at pictures of Ambrose and the family?"

He nodded.

"Well, it does more than just show pictures. It connects to libraries and museums and other places of information around the world. Like using a telephone but with images. You can find out about almost anything."

He looked dubious. "But how do you know what number to ask for? How does the operator know?"

That question took me back a bit. Then I remembered they still had operators in his day and, if I recalled correctly, word and number phrases to connect people. No shortage of phone numbers back then.

"There aren't operators anymore. These communication devices talk to each other."

"That's dafty," he responded with surprise, clearly not believing me.

"As you said, it's been seventy years since you died. Technology is constantly changing. You were with me when my phone talked by itself, and I didn't have to answer it." For a brief moment I was grateful for Winston's spy phone, it made a good example to help Andrew understand our new-fangled technology.

He nodded, recalling the conversation with my "gommy" boss. "Aye, you're right. Things are very different from my time."

"Yes and no. We still have automobiles and airplanes. We're not living on the moon … yet."

"So, being here, on the ship, keeps you from connecting to these information places?" He was still trying to wrap his head around my initial statement.

"Exactly. Tomorrow I'll go across the bay and find a place where the connection is better."

"Not tonight?"

I shook my head. "The place I need to go is closed. I have to wait until the morning."

He accepted the explanation. "Alright then."

"I'm sorry," I offered as weak apology as we left the room and made our way back to the upper decks.

Once again Andrew accompanied me back to my cabin. He entered through the door after Styx and I walked in, like a normal, physical person.

On the table in the sitting room my bag, which I had purposely left behind, was shaking with vibrations. An annoying beep was emitting from the depths. I'm sure my cabin-neighbors hated me at the moment.

I hastily pulled out the phone. "What?" I snapped irritably.

"Why aren't you answering?" he snapped back.

"Because I'm working," I retorted, resisting the urge to slam the phone down on the table. Instead, I placed it next to my bag.

"So have you found out anything?" he demanded.

Entitled rich people have always rubbed me the wrong way. For the millionth time, I wondered why I ever agreed to work with this man. He treated me more like an errant child than an adult who actually held a job and did investigation for a living. It was at that moment, not for the first time in my life, I wished I had a Pulitzer Prize to shove in his smug face.

"You know, Cyrus, I did a fair amount of investigation on my own before I even met you. If you'll recall, I managed to solve the mystery at the Whaley House on my own." The sarcasm was deep and bitter.

"The Whaley House was a minor incident compared to what you are dealing with now," he replied. "There are many different types of hauntings and the one on the Queen Mary is probably the most dangerous of all."

"I know that," I said with some heat. I shivered remembering the thing that tried to take me. Styx's reaction should have clued me in to how bad it was. "I've found the haunted area and talked with several people on the ship," I didn't define whether they were corporeal or spiritual.

Winston didn't ask. He launched into his own findings. "I'm fairly certain it's a demonic haunting, a demon or demons trying to reach through a portal. What I don't understand is how it came about. The age of the ship makes me think this thing could have passed through a long time ago."

Wow, I knew something he didn't. "The area is where the sailors from the Curacoa were lost, their downing must have been an opening. According to the spirits, the thing was kept at bay by a Mister Johnson who said prayers or performed other devotions at least once a week from the time the Queen was opened until his death a few weeks ago. Once he died, the thing has grown stronger. They stopped the paranormal tours when a woman had what management says was an epileptic attack. The ghosts think the thing got to her. She's safe, in case you have a shred of human decency and wondered."

Take that, rich boy!

He ignored the taunt. "Johnson's involvement has only been since the Queen Mary has been in Long Beach," Cyrus pointed out. "If the pivotal incident is the sailors from the Curacoa, then what kept it away from 1942 to 1967?"

"There used to be a cross hung in the room," Andrew recalled. "The Bosun was a spiritual man and it comforted him. Seems like it was serving a double purpose." He smiled.

"And what have you found online?" Winston continued his prodding.

"The connection is pretty bad here. I'm planning on hitting up a coffee shop across the bay to get more information."

"And again, I ask, why is this taking you so long? You've been on the ship for two full days now. Maybe I should contact a spiritualist in the area. They can help you with their expertise. I know there are several very skilled ones in Southern California."

"Why do we need that?" Andrew asked. "Shannon is supposed to be taking care of it, isn't she?"

For a second time I wanted to hug the stuffing out of my uncle for taking my side. "Yeah," I agreed. "Why don't you trust me with this?"

I was irritated that he was going to call in someone with a job description even crazier than mine to help with this. A few weeks ago, I would have been thrilled to have another person assist, or even take over, this type of job. But now I felt I had ownership of the task, I felt I should be the one to complete it.

"That's not the point," Cyrus replied. "It's not a matter of trust but of ability. As I said before, this is not like working with spirits. This is completely different from anything you've encountered before."

"Tell me something I don't know," I grumbled. Against all logic, and knowing that this entity almost consumed me, I was angry that he didn't trust me to complete this assignment. "Why even bother to send me here if I can't do the job? You said I had the ability. You sent me here because you thought I could handle this. So how am I supposed to feel you take me off the case at this point?"

He sighed in exasperation. "I never said I was taking you off. I merely want to send you some help. The lady who usually conducts the paranormal tours is not available, otherwise I would send you to her. This has nothing to do with ability, but with experience. You haven't been on enough of these jobs to deal with a demonic haunting. You have no idea what you're up against, Shannon," his voice was sharp. "This is dangerous."

"Oh, and getting almost shot by a psychopath in San Diego wasn't?" I said just as sharply, referring to my previous investigation. "When I was a reporter, I saw the job through to the end. I'm not about to start crying for help in the middle just because this thing comes from Hell."

"You are purposely not paying attention to what I'm telling you," he said angrily. "As I stated before, you don't know what you're dealing with."

"And this thing doesn't know what it's dealing with," I retorted, my stubbornness meter pegging into the red.

Andrew laughed out loud. "She's got the blood of a Highland warrior in her, Mister Winston. The Scots temper is a powerful thing, especially in a woman."

Cyrus snorted but didn't argue. "Very well, Shannon. But I think you're making a mistake. I'll e-mail you a list of qualified spiritualists, just in case you come to your senses."

"Fair enough," I agreed. The line clicked to signify the end of the call, but I knew he could still monitor me. I wrapped the phone in a hand towel and stuck it in a desk drawer, if he decided to call again at least my neighbors wouldn't be bothered by it.

Andrew was still laughing. "You've definitely got Audrey's temper, lass. She was single-minded as well and when she decided she was going to marry Ambrose there was nothing for it. Her ancestors were Scottish Lairds."

"Well then that makes them my ancestors as well," I said, feeling the adrenaline surge from the argument wearing off and my temper ebbing. I turned and grinned at him. I was so happy for his support, I kept forgetting he was the ghost of a seventeen-year-old boy.

The next morning, I left the Queen Mary parking lot and found myself on the opposite side of the bay in a little coffee bistro with overpriced food and drinks. The internet connection was free with purchase, so I treated myself to a Café Mocha. Amped up coffee and free Wi-Fi were two of my favorite things. Styx had declined my invitation and refused to budge from the overly comfortable king-sized bed. I knew he would make himself scarce when housekeeping came in.

Fast internet connections always gave me a feeling of contentment, as if there were no corner of the world I couldn't investigate. I was in my happy place. The computer was happy as well, chugging along downloading pages and pages of information on demonic hauntings. My previous night's temper was soothed by the fast connection and the caffeine. I scanned through the sites to try and weed out the less informative ones, which actually required some skill on my part since my first reaction to all the pages was to scoff. Tempering my natural cynicism took effort.

Even with the filtering it was a strange collection of documents. I started on one that included a definition of types of hauntings. The subject was presented in a very factual and scientific way, so my BS-meter didn't flare up too much. Even having a definition for some of the happenings in this crazy new job of mine was helpful.

The document I was studying listed three types of hauntings: Residual, Intelligent, and Demonic. The Residual type haunting was the most common and some of what I experienced on the Queen Mary was a good sampling of ghosts that were tied to the location and continued doing what they had done while alive. The 1960s swimming ghost was a prime example of that. She never spoke to me or displayed any interest in the current time frame. She just came in, went swimming, then disappeared. Other types of Residual hauntings are a violent or emotional act that is replayed over and over.

The Intelligent haunting was one where the ghosts were aware of actions going on in their location and even interacted with living. Much like my time at the Whaley House. Anna Whaley knew what had happened in her home and helped me with my investigation. I could not have solved that case without her help. Andrew and the 1930s swimmer were Intelligent hauntings, as were others in the First-Class pool area.

As I read the description of a Demonic haunting, the words of warning from Cyrus Winston echoed in my brain. The article was peppered with phrases like "very dangerous," "incredibly conniving," "immediate action," "do not attempt to remove on your own," "feeds off fear." I remembered that the cheesy ghost show took place a few decks above the forward hull. Yeah, lots of fear and nervous energy just from that alone. Mister Johnson must have done a heck of a job keeping it contained with all that nonsense going on.

After a couple of hours and a couple of mochas I was ready to move on. I had plenty to pour over downloaded on my hard drive, so the ship's internet connection wouldn't affect my research. I asked the barista about local herb shops—not the marijuana kind—and she gave me directions to one fairly close by. Ten minutes later I was parked outside of Splendorous Things, a New Age-y type of establishment with herbs, incense, tie-dye, wind chimes, charms, healing stones, and more. One thing about California beach communities, there were plenty of these types of places around and they wouldn't mind answering weird questions.

Heck, in these places nothing was weird.

"May I help you?" asked the young woman behind the counter.

I took in a deep breath and decided to go for the crazy. "Yeah, I was reading about Demonic hauntings and understand that sage smoke is helpful in dealing this it."

She nodded, understanding. "Yes, the smoke is very cleansing. Let me show you our bundles. How big is the area?"

I breathed a sigh of relief that her manner was business-like. I don't care what your job description is, if you act competent and professional then you will be treated by me as competent and professional. I learned that early on in my reporting years. So many doors were opened to me because I acted like I belonged, and I knew what I was doing.

"About two hundred square feet, I would guess," I answered, following her to the back of the store.

She stopped and turned to me, confusion in her face. "That small? It's not affecting the entire house or building?"

"Not yet. I'm hoping to get rid of it while it's fairly contained."

Nodding, she continued to lead me on. "You're lucky you caught it so early. Are you a demonologist? I don't think I've seen you around."

"No, I'm new here and I'm kind of an amateur. But I've been reading up and want to get as many things prepared as I can. I'm sure I'll benefit from having a professional help me out." My tirade at Winston last night seemed hollow as I admitted to my lack of experience and the consideration of getting someone to help. *Hypocrite*, I thought to myself.

"I'll be happy to recommend someone from the area. With that old ship in the bay, we have lots of paranormal activity in this town. The energy from it seems to draw the spirits in." She smiled.

I smiled back. *Certainly good for business.*

We stopped at the back wall which was filled with herbs dried in bundles or in little bottles and other containers. With all the different varieties, the scent was actually nice. She picked up a small bundle of sage wrapped tightly with twine.

"For your area you might only need two to three branches. Do you know the procedure?"

"I just light the branches and wave them around, don't I?" I kind of assumed no instructions were needed.

"Actually, it's more than that," she said in a helpful manner. "The Native American ritual requires circulating the smoke with a turkey feather. If you put the sage pieces in a small receptacle to burn, you can use the feather to direct the smoke to the areas that need it."

"Oh, okay. Thanks."

The phrase "you learn something new every day" had a completely unique interpretation in my new line of work. I returned to the ship armed with my sage, a shell to burn the leaves, a turkey feather, and a business card with a couple of demonologists written on the back.

Having skipped breakfast, I enjoyed a casual meal in the diner on the main deck. Living the life of a loner, I've gotten used to the sidelong glances and even looks of pity from those around me as our culture has a problem with women who dine alone. It's never bothered me since my objective is to eat a meal and I don't particularly care if I'm accompanied or not. Technology has been helpful since all I need to do is get out my cell phone and I'm instantly connected, so I guess that keeps me from looking too pathetic to others. Whatever.

Neither Styx nor Andrew were visible in my cabin when I returned. I never made the assumption that either of them were gone, just not visible. I unloaded my bag with my new purchases and prepared the materials for a smudging of the forward hull area. For such a small area I chose two stems of sage from the bundle, folding them to fit inside the shell. My lighter, the legacy of my smoking days and too useful to give up, was transferred from my bag to my jacket pocket along with the feather. Thusly fortified, I made my way down into the depths of the Queen Mary to perform the ritual that I hoped would encourage The Darkness to move on.

The advantage of having a crew of ghostly helpers on this assignment was the assurance that certain that doors would be unlocked and stairwells accessible for my wanderings. I was grateful that it was a weekday during the off-season and the staff on the ship was minimal because I never ran into any of them when I walked through the spaces that were supposed to be off-limits to tourists. Since I've never subscribed to luck or fate, I chalked it up to "spiritual intervention."

Outside the doorway where The Darkness lurked, Styx was calmly sitting as if waiting for me. I interrupted him in mid-grooming of his lower back, which he quickly stopped when he saw me. With a silent meow, he rose to his feet and walked towards me, rubbing against my legs and purring.

"Thanks for the vote of confidence," I said to him. "I sure hope this works." I began pulling out the shell, leaves, and feather and put them on the floor. Kneeling over my ingredients, I shredded some of the sage leaves into the shell then lit them with my lighter. The pungent smoke rolled up from the burning leaves and Styx sneezed.

"Bless you." I picked up the shell with its smoky contents and began pushing the smoke in front of me with the feather. I crossed the threshold of the room and stirred the smoke directly into the area where The Darkness felt strongest. Back and forth I crossed the room again and again, stirring the sage smoke all around me and the space.

By the time I was done my eyes were watering and I stunk of burnt sage. Styx, being the more intelligent of the two of us, stayed out of the room but watched my motions carefully. As the smoke dissipated through the cracks and crevices, it felt slightly lighter and less oppressive. Had the smudging worked?

I stood next to the rickety wooden chair and let my senses search for any changes. The evil was still lurking, but it had drawn back in the face of the smoke. A respite, not a reversal. I sighed and sank into the wooden chair that was the only object in the room, steadying myself as it wobbled on uneven legs.

Suddenly, I was looking down on the room from a vantage point in the ceiling. A man with thinning hair and a thickening waistline was sitting in the chair. From the style of his suit, I put the time frame at around the late 1960s or early 1970s. Wide lapels on the jacket and a wide, and very bright, tie. Definitely around the time The Queen began her service to Long Beach as a tourist attraction. The man in the chair had to be Mister Johnson, slighter older than the young man who was shipped off to war almost thirty years ago from this time.

I followed the man's gaze to the section of the hull where The Darkness originated, but the presence could barely be felt, and it certainly wasn't as powerful as it was in my time. Using whatever means I had to propel myself, I moved so that I was next to the man who had done so much to keep this evil contained. On closer inspection, I could see the gray at his temples and the beginning of cheek jowls as his mouth moved to form the words of a quiet prayer. A prayer directed to the wall before his chair which had been the site of the accident so many, many years ago.

"In the name of Jesus, I rebuke you, Spirit. I command you to go directly from here, without manifestation and without harm to me or anyone, to Heaven so that you can be disposed according to the Holy Will."

He crossed himself and began again, the same prayer. I could feel the force of his will against The Darkness. The words were barely audible but the power behind them was evident. He was calmly and firmly ordering this evil thing to leave. Something he would continue to do for the rest of his life.

With a lurch I was back in my own time, sitting in the same but older chair. Styx was standing in my lap; he must have jumped up there and broken my connection. His eyes wide and bright green staring into my own. I stroked his head for comfort, and he pressed the top of it into my palm, purring.

"I'm sorry it took so long for someone to believe you, Mr. Johnson," I said quietly to the room. "No one will ever know how hard you worked to keep this thing contained."

The words faded away in the empty room. Moving Styx off my lap, I got stiffly to my feet. Inwardly, I had to admit Cyrus Winston was correct that this assignment might be beyond me.

No, my stubborn inner voice cried. *You're not giving up yet.*

CHAPTER 6

I made my way slowly to the main part of the ship, leaving Styx to find his own hidden path back to our cabin. I put the shell with the sage ashes in the bathroom with the fan on to dissipate the smoke smell since I had a no-smoking cabin, and I didn't want to be a hypocrite. Although I was sure there was at least four decades of tobacco smoke locked behind the paint and wallpaper.

"Well, the smudge only did a smidge of good," I said with a sigh, falling back onto the softness of the down-filled, duvet-covered bed. I stared up at the ceiling until a black fuzzy face blocked my view. Styx's sandpaper tongue rasped across my cheek before he moved down to lay next to my midsection.

Andrew coalesced into view. "Aye," he agreed. "It is a bit of a puzzle."

I rolled onto my side where I could see him contorting his lanky body to sit in one of the chairs beside the bed. I wondered why he bothered, but I guess habits die hard — literally in his case.

I said nothing for several moments, my mind searching to put a reason to the how and why of The Darkness. I knew where it sprang from, and I knew what it took to keep it at bay. Then Cyrus Winston's words came back to me from our last phone conversation.

"You said the Bosun kept a cross in that room, didn't you?" I asked Andrew. "Could that be the solution to the problem? Just put another cross in there?"

"That was long ago," replied Andrew. "And the ship was still in service, sailing between England and New York. It's much, much stronger than it was back then."

"So, keeping the Queen in one place has actually contributed to this thing growing?"

"As far as I can tell. Then again, I was with my boilers most of the time. But as long as I've been here it's never felt so powerful."

"I wonder what would happen if we just did nothing and let it go?" I mused, only half seriously.

"That'd be daft of you," he said quickly. "And I don't think that's a good plan at all. Remember, you were the one down on your backside when you confronted it."

I shivered at the memory. "Point taken," I conceded. "Plus, the poor woman who it attacked; I can't let that happen again. But what makes it grow? What does it feed off?"

"Energy, I think," Andrew offered. "Spiritual energy. When the accident happened, and all those poor souls drowned it created a lot of energy. I even felt it where I was down in the lower decks. And with all the spirits on this ship, we have a frightful amount of it."

"So why did Mister Johnson's praying make it weaker? Isn't there energy in prayer? Shouldn't it have made it stronger?"

"Mister Johnson was fighting it with his spiritual faith. Same as the Bosun who used that room before and after the accident. He was man of faith."

I sat up and swung my legs around to face him. "What's the difference between spiritual energy and spiritual faith? Aren't they the same thing?"

He laughed at the comment. "You must have missed a lot of church services when you were a lass," he said with a chuckle.

"I'm a Heathen," I quipped my favorite response to religious discussions.

His face lost its humor. Churchgoing was a strong ritual during his life, and one did not treat religion so cavalierly. "Are you now?"

"Sorry," I apologized. "It's a joke. I'm not really. But you're right that I didn't spend much time in church. Explain the difference to me," I prodded him to get off the uncomfortable direction we were heading.

He looked askance at me not sure what was true and what was folly, but he answered directly. "The difference is that everyone, be they living or spirit, has spiritual energy. But not everyone has spiritual faith. Mister Johnson believed in his words. His faith was so strong it created a wall that the thing couldn't breech."

"So, it was his faith, his conviction in what he was doing, that held it back," I surmised.

Andrew nodded. "Faith is a powerful thing. You'd know that if you went to church more."

I didn't respond to his scolding but slid off the bed and walked over to my computer, pulling it out of sleep mode. "I remember reading about confronting these things with firmness, conviction. Let me see if I can find the article…"

Two hours later, I finally looked up from the screen. Reading through endless documents that your rational mind considers bunk, but your present situation demands you find a solution amidst that bunk can cause extreme drowsiness. A drowsiness that requires more than in-room coffee. As my chin drooped on my chest for the second time in twenty minutes, I knew I had to get up and walk around to wake myself up.

Andrew had left during that time, probably because when I'm researching, I tend to block out everything else. He was probably down in the First-Class pool area offering what comfort he could to his fellow spirits. On more than one occasion I was grateful for his faith in me, and I owed it to him, and all the other ghosts, to find an answer. The smudging was only a temporary fix, much like Mister Johnson's prayers. I needed to find something more permanent.

Styx was asleep in the exact middle of the bed as I gathered my bag from the bedside table where I had left it after removing my smudging supplies. It was a perfect position because I couldn't touch him from any of the open sides of the bed. It was his Do Not Disturb in physical form.

"I'm heading out for a walk," I told him from the doorway of the bedroom. His ear flicked in response which was all the acknowledgement I was going to get. I smiled as I exited the cabin and strode down the hallway to the stairs. I kind of enjoyed our communication, or lack thereof. It was a pretty easy relationship, definitely much easier than my human interactions.

As I walked around the decks my mind recalled all the documents I had downloaded about Demonic Hauntings. My past two hours of reading only cemented what I had gathered when I first read it at the coffee shop, nothing about these types of hauntings was good.

Temperature drop in the location?

Check.

Feelings of helplessness and sadness?

Check.

A sense of evil?

Double check.

Change in a person's behavior?

Well, there was the woman who had a "seizure" on the paranormal tour, so I would definitely count that as a check.

Pets who become frightened or angry in that area?

Oh, a big check for that one. The vision of Styx all puffed up and hissing when The Darkness almost had me was etched into my memory. I had never seen him act like that before. That reaction alone should have warned me that this Darkness was something powerful and investigative skills alone would not defeat it.

I wandered for an hour or so, then returned to the room to change for dinner. I needed to chew on more than my thoughts, so the steakhouse would be my dinner again. Some combination of my walk and the smell of the bay was making me hungry, but my side dishes would meet my doctor's approval post-heart attack.

That night, I tried to sleep but my dreams were becoming nightmares. I found myself within The Darkness again and fighting to keep my sense of self. The suffocation in that inky nothingness was almost too real and I tossed and turned, trying to escape it. My dream-self was cringing in fear, terrified of the lack of any sensation. The sounds of the screaming, drowning sailors intensified but I couldn't move my hands to put them over my ears in an effort to block it.

Malevolent was a good word to describe it. Evil seemed to permeate it and as it grew its appetite also increased. The spirits in the First-Class pool were easy prey for this demon, although it had shown a taste for the living as evidenced by the woman who fainted on the midnight ghost tour. Mister Johnson was vindicated in his opinion that the drowned men of the Curacao had created a portal for this thing to pass through. The man's dedication to keeping it under control during his life made me admire him all the more. He was a soldier fighting a war up until the day he died. Too bad no one took his warning seriously.

As I was gasping for breath, the screams of the men were drowned by the high-pitched screech of a young child. Like fingernails on a blackboard, the sound made me cringe. How did a child get caught by this thing? Then my mind flashed to ghosts of the young children lost on this ship. The Darkness had one of them.

I was instantly awake, sitting up and still trying to breath—although it was easier now. Emotions cascaded over me like a waterfall. Pain. Fear. Anxiety. Confusion. And anger. Anger that I had failed to protect one of the children. At least I had in my dream. I threw off the covers, disturbing Styx who was sleeping next to me. He watched as I threw on clothes, slipped into my shoes with no socks, grabbed my flashlight, and bolted out of the cabin. I had to make sure the spirits were alright.

To my horror, my dream-nightmare was correct. Jackie was missing from the assembled ghosts who were nervously huddled near the door of the Bosun's Locker. Andrew had his flat cap in his hands, wringing it with worry.

"She's gone," I supplied the words they couldn't. "Jackie's been taken."

He nodded mutely. I looked into the room and saw her translucent teddy bear on the floor. The demon had intruded further into the room and was half-way to the door. Anger made me see red and I boldly stepped up to it. There would be a reckoning. I was angry and I would fight with this thing to get Jackie back from wherever it had taken her.

I was seeing red as I stood before it, but The Darkness just laughed at me—or whatever passed for a laugh. I felt its emotions clearly as it enveloped me, and the weight of the crushing darkness enfolded me. Just like my dream, but here in reality I could feel my fists clench as I braced for this battle. That was exactly the wrong thing to do. Almost too late I realized that strong emotions were like a pathway for this thing. My anger only fueled its power.

I mentally put a brake on my anger, not an easy thing to do when you're being sucked into a portal of evil, and calmed myself, silently thanking Rachel for recommending meditation after my almost death.

Queen for a Night

CHAPTER 7

I focused my entire concentration against the darkness that surrounded me. I had no concept of where I was or how long we battled, because it was definitely a battle of wills. I stood firm in my purpose that the entity had to leave. Just like Mister Johnson before me, I wasn't mad, and I wasn't angry. I was firm but unyielding.

The entity was probing me, looking for weak spots or any place it could find a chink in my armor of self-confidence. It was dank and musty smelling; the odor of dead and dying things. It was dark, entirely dark; dark without any sense of feeling or connecting. I was isolated from all around me as I battled. But being alone and standing up for myself was something I had done almost all my life. Who else took on the rich and privileged for the sake of the common person? Who else wouldn't take "no" for an answer? What better warrior than someone who has confronted human evil many times during her life. The very core of my being resonated with a need to see justice done, to see people get a fair deal, to right wrongs and help the good guy win. What difference did it make where the evil originated from? I would fight it until my dying breath.

Of course, my dying is exactly what this thing wanted. When I had met it the first time, I had no idea what it was capable of. Now I was armed with knowledge of my first encounter and the fact that it held Jackie hostage; I would not bend to its will. I used my own will as a shield to protect me. Not only me, but the ghosts and the visitors who were susceptible to its power. I fought on.

Time had no meaning in this empty arena of battle. I had no concept of how long we fought. Was it a day? A month? A year? The power of darkness against a stubborn Scots temper. But it was stubbornness without emotion. I wouldn't feed this thing what it wanted.

Go away. Go away. Go away. Go away, I chanted my mantra over and over and over. The instructions said not to be angry, that a strong, reactive emotion would give it an opening to invade me. I focused on maintaining my calm demeanor and repeating my chant.

The entity backed off from its push, as if confounded by the force of my appeal. I made the mistake of seeing this as a retreat and I relaxed for a fraction of a second. Wrong move on my part. Falling for its feint, The Darkness doubled its efforts and slammed into me with such force that I probably would have fallen if I could have felt anything around me. I mentally gasped at the impact while it used my hesitation to get past my defense.

I was overcome with feelings of failure. How could I, a mere mortal, think I had the power to go up against something that had been born at the beginning of time? I was a puny, worthless insect and my words were incoherent mumbling. I felt cold, so very, very cold, and drained of all my energy. I just wanted to lay down and sleep, forget this unwinnable confrontation. Just relax, give up, surrender my will to The Darkness. An image of Styx was suddenly in my mind. He was crying at me, trying to keep me from falling into that deadly slumber. If this evil prevailed then who would there be to help him, to help the ghosts? I saw Mister Johnson again, sitting on his chair, facing this entity all alone with only his prayer as sword and shield. He was one man, but he succeeded in holding it at bay.

Finding the strength I needed, I redoubled my efforts and cast aside any thoughts of sleep and peace, urging myself to continue this confrontation. I dialed my will power up to eleven and focused it like a laser beam on this thing. Faith and conviction, just like Mister Johnson.

YOU DON'T BELONG HERE.

GO AWAY.

LEAVE THIS PLACE.

GO AWAY.

I CAST YOU OUT.

GO AWAY.

Andrew told me later that I had, in fact, fallen to the floor when the thing attacked. Styx calmly climbed up on me and lay down on my chest. No fuzzing out, no hissing; just calm and quiet. The other ghosts who had been watching formed a circle around me, hands clasped, and lent their strength to mine.

From my perspective, all I felt was a new wave of energy that allowed me to push back at The Darkness. And anyone who's met me knows that I'm pretty damn pushy. This was the final stand, no more keeping it at bay. I had to get this entity off the ship for good.

I had to do it for me.

I had to do it for Styx.

I had to do it for Andrew.

I had to do it for all the ghosts.

I had to do it for all the visitors – past, present, and future.

But most of all, I had to do it for Mister Johnson who dedicated most of his life to keeping this in control. His sacrifice had helped so many people for so long he was overdue for some help in this fight.

And most importantly, I had to do this for Jackie and get her back to this plane of existence.

I continued my chant, increasing the volume in my head, willing this thing to be gone with every ounce of energy I could muster. I placed my faith in the rightness of my actions, that this entity was an intruder and did not deserve to be here.

Was that a faint trace of light in the darkness? Yes! I could see the dark starting to fade from inky black to deep gray. Buoyed by this discovery I set my will directly against it, a small chink in this thing's armor. I kept up the chant, using my stubbornness but not my anger.

YOU DON'T BELONG HERE.

GO AWAY.

LEAVE THIS PLACE.

GO AWAY.

I CAST YOU OUT.

GO AWAY.

Deep gray faded to gray. Gray faded to light gray. The light gray, like a fog, began to dissipate and suddenly I could see Jackie within it. I reached out to her and she came to me, holding onto me in this strange limbo. Everything around us continued to fade and soon it was white. There was nothing left to fight. It was done.

Wearily I opened my eyes and saw Styx on my chest. I was so weak, he felt like Thor's hammer holding me down so I couldn't sit up. His neon green eyes faded back to their normal color, and he rubbed his head against my chin, a cat's version of the fist-bump. With a quick lick on my cheek, he got down. Slowly, painfully I sat up. It was then I noticed all the ghosts in a ring around me with Jackie sitting by my head, crying.

"It's okay," I reassured her. "You're back."

Jackie nodded and stood up, tears streaming down her cheeks. The Lady in White was next to her, giving her teddy back. The girl squeezed it tight, rubbing her wet face into it.

"And thank you," I wheeze, looking at the spirits surrounding me. "You helped. A lot." The relief I felt was palpable, and I could feel their relief as well. The room was no longer freezing.

I scooted back, leaning against the wall; I didn't trust my legs to hold me if I tried to stand. I was shaking like a leaf, but the ordeal was over. The Darkness was gone, I was still here, and ghosts were smiling.

"That was fantastic," grinned Andrew, kneeling next to me. "The power of a stubborn Scots against a demon—the poor thing didn't stand a chance. You are definitely Audrey's granddaughter, I'll give you that." I nodded because my voice had run out. Styx immediately got into my lap, leaning against me as if trying to share his strength. His purr was loud and deep, resonating against my chest, and it actually made me feel a little better.

As much as Andrew and the other ghosts wanted to help me to my room, it just wouldn't happen that way. I eventually dragged myself up and out, slow painful step after slow painful step. Back in my room with the DO NOT DISTURB sign posted, I collapsed on the bed and closed my eyes.

It was mid-day when I opened them again. Both Styx and Andrew were watching me with concern. I smiled weakly at them, sitting up and fluffing pillows so I could rest my back against the headboard. I didn't realize that a mental battle would be so physically draining. I reached for the room phone. "Food and coffee first," I stated.

Getting dressed took twice as long as normal but I had just finished when nourishment arrived. Andrew had a wicked look in his eyes like he wanted to answer the knock, but my scowl made him stop half-way to the door. The service person might drop my coffee and that wouldn't do.

"So now what will you be doing?" he asked as I poured my second cup and shared a piece of bacon with Styx.

"Going back to the old homestead in Idyllwild," I answered. "It seems to be my resting place in between these jobs. It will be nice to see Nana Mac again, and she'll want to hear all about what happened."

He nodded but didn't reply.

CHAPTER 8

The next day was Sunday and I managed to get myself up and get dressed to attend the Brunch that everyone had been raving about. As I draped a necklace over my head, the phone call I was waiting for came. It was Cyrus Winston, and he was as mad as a wet hen. Not that I know anything about hens, wet or otherwise.

"That was without a doubt the riskiest thing you could have done, Miss MacIntyre. The severity of the situation called for a professional, not an amateur with little knowledge of what she was up against." No greeting, no concern for my well-being, just a launch into his scolding.

"And you are a pompous, over-controlling, egomaniac, Mister Winston." I replied with as much heat. "I am not your servant or your soldier. I do not have to obey your orders."

"You accepted this job and all it entails. I expect you to use the resources you are given." He obviously had a burr up his butt about my going solo against the demon. He might have been right, but I had succeeded and that only made me angrier.

"Yes, I accepted the job, but I never agreed to be on a leash. Just because I accepted this James Bond phone does not give you the right to spy on me any time you feel like it."

"The transmitter was a precaution in case you were unable to reach the phone. It was for your protection."

"You're running a fine line between protection and the ultimate in micromanagement. I can just as easily quit this gig. I don't have to stay." After what I just survived, I wouldn't let anyone attack me like this. "There are plenty of others who would be happy to chain themselves to you for the money. Besides, if you're as 'gifted' as I am, why don't you get up off your rich ass and do this work yourself."

There was silence on the line. I realized too late I had overstepped my bounds big time and he didn't deserve the rebuke. But when my stubborn side is drawn out, it's sometimes hard to put it back. It's made my life hard on many occasions, and why I was such a good journalist.

I heard him sigh; it sounded both hurt and resigned. "Very well. I'll create a voice recognition app that will turn the two-way on at the sound of your voice. Will that calm your ire, Shannon?"

The use of my first name implied he was back to business.

"Yes," I answered in a more subdued voice. "Thank you." I added, as Mom always reminded me that you should thank people who are doing you a favor. Even if I was still mad at him. I heard the line close, and we were done.

As I walked along the deck to the brunch location. There were crowds of people in formal, and not so formal, attire. An Event List nearby showed about eight different wedding receptions going on. Heck, if I had the funds and the inclination to get married, the Queen Mary would be a fantastic place to do it.

In a cramped elevator, I was surrounded by young adults in ill-fitting suits and dresses and even worse language. The F-word was scattered through the conversation so casually it had ceased to be "bad" for this generation. How sad, I thought to myself, thinking of the truly classy people who had been aboard this ship. Royalty, famous actors and statesmen, people who put the class in First-Class. Now it was inhabited by gum-chewing kids playing at being grown up. I was relieved when my stop was the first.

When did I become such a grumpy old lady? I asked myself. Next thing I know I'll be shouting at them to get off the lawn. I shrugged and made my way to the restaurant and the pleasure of a grand buffet in grand surroundings.

And grand it was! Table after table of food items from around the world—American, Asian, Latin and, of course, lots of champagne. I stopped after my second glass knowing I had a long drive back to Idyllwild. My dieting went out the window as I helped myself to a little of everything, including dessert. So what if I gained a couple of pounds on this alone? I knew my sister would be getting me healthy again once I was back at the homestead. I ate slowly savoring each and every bite. I knew full well not every job would come with such rich perks, so I made the most of it.

After the meal and stuffed to the brim, I lurched back to my cabin still aching from my battle with The Darkness. The oppressive air I had been sensing was gone completely and the ghosts were at peace again. Silently, I again thanked Mister Johnson for the incredible job he had done keeping the evil at bay.

When I opened the door to my room, I saw the inky blackness of my furry partner amidst the tumble of sheets and blankets. Housekeeping wouldn't come until I checked out, so the bed was still a rumpled mess. His head came up immediately as I approached, smelling the treat I had brought him—a napkin with a couple of shrimp I smuggled out of the buffet. In my mind, he had earned it. As I leaned over to put it on the floor, he immediately jumped off the bed and started in on them.

"Enjoy them, buddy," I told him with a smile, then I straightened up and went to the closet, pulling out my duffle bag. I changed out of my nice clothes into my jeans and shirt, then packed up my belongings.

Once everything was complete, I looked at my watch to make sure I still had time.

Checkout was at noon, so I was good. Pulling out a piece of stationary from the desk, I sat down and penned a note to the "regular psychic" on the ship.

"You were away when I was on board, but I wanted to let you know the ghosts on the ship were extremely helpful in ridding the lower decks of a demonic haunting. It's probably already up on the Winston's Mysteries web site by the time you read this.

"*Apparently the loss of Mr. Johnson allowed a dark entity to board through the souls of the drowned sailors of the Curacoa. Mr. Johnson had been keeping it contained with once-a-week visits where he would recite scripture and pray. His faith and strength of will were key to his success. The ghosts greatly admired his dedication. Other than that, things are back to normal.*

Sincerely Yours – "

I signed my penname, folded the letter, found a matching envelope, put the note in, and sealed it. Carefully I printed her name on the front. One of the weirdest letters I'd ever written, but she would understand. I dropped it off at the check-in counter on my way out.

Duffel on one shoulder and cat securely stashed in my bag on the other, I left the Queen Mary hopefully in better shape than when I found her. At my car I put the bag with Styx in first so he could get out, then I moved to the trunk to load my single piece of luggage. I felt bad that I hadn't seen Andrew to say good-bye; I wanted to tell him how much his help and support meant. I really couldn't have done the job without him.

My car had just exited to the freeway when a shimmering apparition appeared in the back seat. I saw it from my rear-view mirror and almost ran off the road, swinging the steering wheel quickly to avoid the shoulder. The shape formed into Andrew with a wide grin, smiling at me.

"So, are we going back to my brother's house?" he asked calmly.

"What?! How? Huh?" I could only sputter. My eyes were quickly switching from rear view mirror to front view, hoping I wouldn't get in an accident. I was completely dumbfounded by his appearance.

"I decided to come with you," he explained. "Meeting you made me realize how much I missed my family. I know Ambrose is gone and didn't stay back, but you said Audrey was still at the house, and I had a mind to see her." He was oh so matter of fact as if he did this every day.

"But...but..." I struggled with some preconceived notions I had about ghosts and being tied to a place. "I thought you had to stay with the ship?"

"Well, most spirits do because it's familiar to them. But since almost all of the boilers were removed, I really don't have the tie that I used to. You and me being family, we have a strong connection and that allows me to go with you." He smiled broadly. "So here I am."

After almost sideswiping a car next to me I decided it would be best to keep my eyes looking forward for driving. To say I was shocked was an understatement. I never imagined taking a ghost home as a souvenir.

Not knowing what else to say, I shrugged and replied, "Welcome aboard."

EPILOG

I settled into my bed, actually glad to be back at the house, which was a rare feeling for me.

Styx was performing his nightly grooming ritual, using my legs to keep himself from falling over as he stretched his limbs into impossible positions. I had concluded after watching this feat that cats are boneless.

Andrew had disappeared the moment we rolled up the drive. I figured he would find his own way around and didn't worry about it. However, I did warn my sister I had brought a stray home. She understood and was actually thrilled that I had found family, even if it was a spirit. We found some time after the kids had gone to bed for me to recount my adventure to her and Dan, because none of us felt secure letting the kids in on what their aunt did. It all seemed so crazy, although I secretly felt they would think it was cool.

My body still ached, and I hoped for a respite before starting another assignment. If it was anything like the last one, I would need time to recover before confronting something similar to what I had just experienced. The weight of Styx moved off my leg and I shifted to a more comfortable position on my side.

As my eyelids drooped and I relaxed, welcoming the peaceful sleep, I blearily saw ghostly figures appear beside my bed. Nana Mac and Andrew.

"Bless you, Shannon," my grandmother said with a catch in her voice. "Bless you for bringing Andrew home."

This house had never been Andrew's home, but I was too tired to make the point.

"Uh-huh," I mumbled. "You're welcome, Nana Mac." My voice faded as I drifted into my slumber, glad to be in my space surrounded by family.

About The Queen Mary

In December of 1930, hull number 543 was laid at the John Brown Shipyards in Clydebank, Scotland. This was the start of the Queen Mary, the most luxurious liner ever designed. Unfortunately, the Great Depression spilled over into European economies and the ship's building was delayed as the Cunard Line looked for other funding. In January 1934, the Cunard Steamship Company eventually merged with the White Star Line, creating Cunard White Star, LTD. In March of that year, the British Treasury advanced the company £4,500,000 to complete the ship.

With only the hull and outer plates, the ship was launched and christened THE QUEEN MARY by Her Majesty Queen Mary (wife of King George V) in September of 1934. Afterwards the ship was transferred to a fitting out basin where the rest of the building could be completed. She took her maiden voyage in May 1936.

The Yarrow boilers that powered the ship were a feat of engineering for their time and allowed the Queen to cruise at 28.5 knots. She set a speed record in August of that year with an average speed over 30 knots. She set another record in 1938 for an average speed of 31 knots.

Her last peacetime cruise was in August of 1939, when she arrived in New York. Germany had invaded Poland and the war had begun for Europe. She stayed in New York while she was retrofitted as a troop carrier, complete with gray paint to make her less detectible. This earned her the nickname the Grey Ghost. She transported almost 800,000 troops during the war, setting a passenger record of 16,082 American troops aboard on a single trip. Adolph Hitler offered a $250,000 reward and the Iron Cross to any U-boat captain who could sink her. Winston Churchill was a passenger three times during the war, and it's rumored he planned the Battle of Normandy while on board. After the war, she helped transport war brides and their children to the U.S.

The Queen Mary was returned to passenger service in July 1947. Many upgrades were made to the ship while she was restored to her former glory. By the 1960s, air travel had surpassed cruise ships for long distance transportation. The Queen Mary was auctioned off in 1967 and avoided being turned to scrap. The city of Long Beach, California bought her to become an attraction for the city. Her last voyage was in September of that year, taking the long route around Cape Horn as the Queen was too wide for the Panama Canal.

The Queen Mary has had several owners over the years, including the Walt Disney Company, since she first found her berth in Long Beach and there have been several groups dedicated to preserving her glorious history. In 2006, the RMS Queen Mary 2 saluted her predecessor by blowing her horns as she made her way to port in Los Angeles. The original Queen Mary replied using her one working horn. It was a historic meeting.

Today the Queen Mary is a resort hotel, a popular place for weddings and receptions, business meetings, fine dining, and casual meet ups. Restoration is ongoing and many of the First-Class bars and lounges have been restored to give modern visitors a taste of the past.

The Ghosts and Haunted Locations on the Queen Mary

Lady in White — In what is now the Observation Lounge, a beautiful young woman in an elegant white evening gown has been reported dancing alone in a shadowy corner of the salon, which used to be the ship's First-Class lounge. Another mysterious woman in white has been seen close to the front desk. She will usually disappear behind a pillar. There are signs on the ship indicating where these spirits have appeared.

John Pedder — John was an 18-year-old crewman who was crushed by watertight door number 13 during a drill in 1966. He has often been seen walking along Shaft Alley before disappearing by door number 13.

William Stark — Senior second officer was accidentally poisoned in 1949 when he drank tetrachloride that the captain kept in an old gin bottle.

Jackie — Jackie is a little girl seen and heard in the First-Class pool area. While it's recorded that she drowned in the Second-Class pool during the ship's sailing, her voice and the sound of laughter have been recorded in First-Class area.

First-Class Swimming Pool Area — This area is one of the most haunted on the ship. Wet footprints mysteriously appear leading from the deck of the pool to the changing rooms, and ladies in period bathing suits have been seen stopping by for a swim even though the pool has been closed for more than 30 years. There have also been reports of seeing the spirit of a young girl carrying her teddy bear along with disembodied voices, laughter, and splashing sounds.

Cabin B340 — This cabin has so much activity that it is no longer booked as a hotel room. People who stayed in this room in the past reported their covers being violently pulled off the bed and the water facets turning on in the middle of the night. Every time the room was rented out, the guests would call the front desk during the night to request another room.

Front Hull/Bosun's Locker — Tearing metal, rushing water, screaming, and pounding of the drowned sailors from the Curacao (pronounced keer-a-sow) can be heard in this area of the ship. The Queen cut the ship in half when it got in her way during her time as a troop transport ship in World War II. Over 200 men died in the accident.

AUTHOR'S NOTE

The prayer recited by Mr. Johnson is a paraphrasing of the Catholic Prayer Against Evil.

Writing this story has been an absolute joy and I'm so glad you're finally able to read it. The picture on the front cover is one I took when I visited The Queen Mary for research, and you can tell by Shannon's descriptions that it is a gorgeous ship. I wasn't able to stay overnight, but I did stand outside of the Cabin B340 and it is indeed creepy.

The incident with Shannon being the only person for the general tour is actually what happened to me, but it was a stroke of luck because I was able to spend time in the First-Class Pool area. As the saying goes, truth is often stranger than fiction. And it's even better when I can incorporate it into the story.

Thanks for reading.

Donna Keeley, November 2022

Made in the USA
Columbia, SC
24 May 2023